BY REASON
OF INSANITY

David Brunelle Legal Thriller #3

STEPHEN PENNER

ISBN-13: 978-0615821658
ISBN-10: 0615821650

By Reason of Insanity

Joy Lorton, Editor.
Cover by Nathan Wampler Book Covers.

THE DAVID BRUNELLE LEGAL THRILLERS

BY REASON
OF INSANITY

In addition to the plea of not guilty, the defendant may enter a plea of insanity existing at the time of the act charged.

Insanity existing at the time of the act charged is a defense to the crime of murder.

For a defendant to be found not guilty by reason of insanity you must find that, as a result of mental disease or defect, the defendant's mind was affected to such an extent that the defendant was unable to perceive the nature and quality of the acts with which the defendant is charged or was unable to tell right from wrong with reference to the particular acts with which the defendant is charged.

State of Washington
Pattern Criminal Jury Instruction 20.01

CHAPTER 1

"Holy Mother of God."

Dave Brunelle, King County homicide prosecutor, stepped into the bedroom of the West Seattle craftsman and surveyed the carnage.

Seattle P.D. detective Larry Chen turned around from where he was supervising the processing of the scene. His large frame seemed uncomfortable in the small room. "There's nothing holy here, Dave," he said. "And it's hard to see God at work in this." He glanced around the room. "More like the other guy."

Blood spatter covered the walls, slashes of red reaching for the ceiling, their contents dripping to the floor. One side of the queen bed was absolutely soaked in blackish blood, the sheets and blankets cascading to the wooden floor in a scarlet waterfall. Three forensics officers were photographing the scene and collecting evidence, their camera flashes blasting the gore with a sickening strobe. The stench of death permeated the confines of the stuffy room.

"You got the mother part right, though," said Chen. "She was the mother."

"Who? The victim?" Brunelle asked, trying to wrap his mind around what his eyes were seeing.

"Yep." Chen gestured to the blood-soaked indentation on the bed. "This is mom's room."

Brunelle stepped toward the bed and frowned. "So where's the body?"

"We had to get it out of here," Chen said. "Some of the boys were getting sick."

Brunelle considered what could be so bad that seasoned police officers needed to have the body removed before they could finish their work. "What happened?"

"Well, we're still piecing it together," Chen answered. He chuckled darkly. "So to speak."

Brunelle didn't understand the joke. He shook his head at his friend.

"Her face was hacked to pieces," Chen explained. "With a hatchet. The medical examiner guessed at least twenty times, directly to the face. Probably started where the bridge of her nose used to be."

"Probably?"

Chen shrugged. "There wasn't much face left."

Brunelle looked up at the walls again. He wasn't a blood spatter expert, but he'd seen enough to recognize a cast-off pattern. Blood flying off the blade as the killer pulled it back for another blow.

"So, the medical examiner has been and gone already?" Brunelle asked. He tried to sound casual. He should have known Chen wouldn't buy it.

"Yeah. Sorry about that, Romeo." Chen managed a smile at his friend, despite the circumstances. "But don't worry. It wasn't your Kitty-Kat. It was Perkins. He was all business. No flirting at all."

Brunelle nodded, suppressing his own grin. "Ah. Well, that's good, I suppose."

"I thought," Chen teased, "Dr. Anderson might've been laying next to you when I called."

It was shortly after three-thirty in the morning.

"No," Brunelle answered. "We're not quite there yet."

Chen raised an incredulous eyebrow.

"Well, not every night," Brunelle admitted.

"Aha!" One of the forensics techs stood up and pumped a fist. She took a quick picture of something about two feet up the wall nearest the bed, then carefully peeled it off and held it up. Brunelle thought it looked like part of a smashed strawberry.

"I told Ferguson we hadn't found all of her nose," she said. "Here's the last bit."

Obviously not one of the cops who complained about the body, Brunelle thought.

"So, you said she's the mother?" he asked to distract himself from the forensics officer sliding the piece of flesh into a clear evidence baggie. "Whose mother?"

"The killer's," Chen answered.

"She was killed by her own son?" Brunelle questioned.

"Daughter," Chen corrected. "And yes."

Brunelle scolded himself for his sexist assumption. Not because it was sexist; because it was a jump to conclusions without adequate information. "How do you know?"

"Because she's the one who called 911," Chen answered. "She was waiting for us when we got here. Opened the door and showed us right up to the bedroom and everything."

Brunelle's eyebrows shot up. "Wow."

Chen surrendered another dark laugh. "Yeah. Wow is right."

"Where is she now?" Brunelle asked. "Waiting for interrogation back at the precinct?"

"Oh, no." Chen grinned. "She's at Harborview."

"Harborview?" Brunelle asked. Harborview was the aptly named hospital perched on the hill above downtown Seattle.

"Yep," answered Chen. "She's fucking nuts."

CHAPTER 2

Harborview Medical Center was the premiere trauma center for not just Seattle, but the entire Northwest. It was the only Level I trauma center for Washington, Alaska, Montana, and Idaho, and airlift helicopters could routinely be seen flying over the Seattle skyline to land atop the hospital, rushing the most injured patients in the region to the best help available.

It was also the first stop for the mentally ill on their way to involuntary commitment, or criminal charges. Or both.

Brunelle and Chen stepped into the main lobby. The waiting area was filled with all sorts of people nursing all sorts of injuries and ailments. Brunelle knew gunshots and stab wounds were mixed in with croupy kids and dehydrated seniors. Seattle P.D. routinely cross-referenced the Harborview emergency room records against reports of assailants who'd gotten away, but not before being shot and needing medical attention. A man in the corner, wrapped in a dirty blanket and rocking as he muttered to himself, reminded Brunelle why they were there.

"Is she in the psych ward?" he asked.

"Probably," Chen answered. "I had a couple of patrol guys bring her. I imagine that's where she'd end up. Nice lady, except for the crazy part."

"Except for the murdering her mother part," Brunelle added.

Chen grinned. "Yeah, that too."

The psychiatric wing was in the East Clinic, just off the Center Building that dominated the campus. It wasn't a far walk, but the men hurried through the crowded hallways, navigating gurneys of moaning patients, distracted nurses, and residents darting to their next task. The elevator opened for the ninth floor.

"Lingerie, auto parts, homicidal maniacs," Chen quipped.

Brunelle tried not to laugh. He was feeling serious, sometimes difficult around Chen. But he knew he'd be on edge until he could figure out what happened. He couldn't begin thinking about how to present the case to the jury until he knew what to present. And Chen had steadfastly refused to fill him in on the drive over.

"Trust me," he'd said. "You're going to want to hear it directly from her."

'Her' was Keesha Sawyer. A thirty-something woman with short hair, a disarming smile, and an acute case of paranoid schizophrenia.

She was in Room 914, flanked by two police officers and strapped securely to the bed.

"Hello, Detective," she said as Chen and Brunelle entered her room. "Who's your friend?"

"This is Dave Brunelle." Chen gestured toward Brunelle. "He's a prosecutor."

"Oh," Sawyer said, tilting her head back to appraise him. "Are you going to charge me with a crime?"

Brunelle nodded slightly. "We might. I was told you

murdered your mother."

Sawyer smiled. She had a very nice smile. "I murdered her, all right. But it was justified."

Brunelle raised an eyebrow. "If it was justified," he replied, "it's not murder."

Sawyer cocked her head. "Is that right? Well, it was justified all right, so I guess it wasn't murder."

Chen stuck a hand between them, then looked to the patrol officers. "Hey, did you guys read her her rights? I don't want to have this conversation if you didn't Mirandize her."

"No worries, detective," one of the men replied. "I did it in the car, and again when we got here."

Sawyer looked up at the detective, apparently quite at ease with her limbs fastened to the hospital bed. "Oh, don't worry detective. I want to talk. I want to explain."

Brunelle pulled over the one chair in the room and sat down next to her. "Okay. Explain."

Chen pulled a digital recorder from his pocket and placed it on the small tray-table between them.

Sawyer looked at Brunelle for a moment. She seemed very sweet. Kind even. Despite what he'd seen earlier that morning, he was having trouble believing this polite, articulate woman could have hacked her mother's face into oblivion. He didn't fight the feeling. He knew the jury would feel it too. Which is why he needed to hear what she had to say.

"I had to do it," she started. "You have to understand that. It was justified."

"Was she hurting you?" Brunelle asked.

Sawyer smiled broadly. That unhinged twinge from the corner of her eye spread to her mouth. Brunelle hoped she'd testify. The jury would see it too after just a few minutes.

"She wasn't hurting me, Mr. Brunelle. She was murdering me."

Brunelle raised his eyebrows. "Murdering you?"

That's a new one.

"Yes, sir," Sawyer replied earnestly. "Every night. She murdered me in my dreams."

Brunelle pursed his lips. He wasn't a psychologist. He knew a fair amount about various psychoses, but it was from his experience as an advocate. The same experience that trained his mind to break down problems logically and present information linearly. He knew enough to let go of that instinct.

"Explain to me," he coaxed, "how you could be murdered every night in your dreams but still be alive. I don't understand."

Sawyer nodded kindly at him, like a mother explaining something basic to a toddler. "I know, I know. She murdered me in my dreams, but I woke up alive in the morning. I was alive, but I wasn't. I was undead. Do you know what the undead are?"

Brunelle nodded. "Vampires and werewolves, right?"

Sawyer frowned. "Vampires, yes, but not werewolves. Werewolves are very alive."

Brunelle nodded again. "Okay, okay. Sure. So vampires. She turned you into a vampire?"

Not another vampire case, he hoped.

"Of course not, silly," Sawyer laughed. "Vampires aren't real. No, she turned me into a zombie."

Brunelle's eyebrows raised even higher.

"Walking dead," Sawyer explained. "She murdered me in my dreams so that when I woke up I'd be a zombie and she could control me."

Brunelle pressed his fingertips together and placed the index fingers to his lips. "And so that's why you killed her? So she'd stop turning you into a zombie?"

Sawyer shook her head again. "No. I can fight against it. I could stop being a zombie by dinner time. I really like dinner time. Do you like dinner, Mr. Brunelle?"

Brunelle smiled at the sudden question. "Uh, sure. I like dinner."

"Do you cook for yourself, or is there a Mrs. Brunelle?"

Brunelle shook his head. "There's no Mrs. Brunelle."

"Not yet," Chen whispered, but not nearly quietly enough.

Brunelle shot him a glance, then looked back at Keesha Sawyer. "I eat out a lot," he explained.

"Oh, you shouldn't do that," Sawyer admonished. "You don't know what they put in that food. I've been poisoned, did you know that?"

"I didn't know that, Keesha," Brunelle responded. "I'm sorry about that. But can you tell me more about being a zombie. If you could fight it off, why did you have to kill her?"

The smile occasioned by the conversation about dinner melted right off Sawyer's face. It left behind a sorrowful, aghast expression. Wide-eyed, almost terrified. "The children," she whispered.

"The children?" Brunelle confirmed.

"Yes, the children," Sawyer answered. "She started to murder the children too."

"What children?" Brunelle asked, as if the woman really had been killing children. He found himself being sucked into Sawyer's reality.

"The children in our complex," Sawyer explained. "The sweetest little children. They laugh and sing and play. Do you have children, Mr. Brunelle?"

Brunelle shook his head curtly. "No, no children." He glared at Chen before he could offer another 'Not yet.'

"That's too bad," Sawyer said. "I bet you'd be a great dad. How old are you, Mr. Brunelle?"

"I'm forty-three," he answered, although he wasn't sure why he felt compelled to answer her questions.

Sawyer shook her head. "Tsk, tsk, Mr. Brunelle. You'd better hurry. Do you at least have a girlfriend? You're a handsome man. I bet you have a girlfriend."

Brunelle glared again at Chen, who grinned but put his hands out to assure he wasn't going to say anything.

"Tell me about the children," Brunelle pressed. "Not my children. The children your mother was going to murder."

Sawyer's face went taut again. Brunelle realized the questions about wives and girlfriends might have been her way of avoiding the topic of her mother murdering the neighborhood kids. Too bad. He needed to hear what she had to say. Before some defense attorney got a hold of it and twisted it into whatever he or she wanted it to mean.

"She wasn't just *going* to murder them, Mr. Brunelle," Sawyer explained. "She had already started. She murdered them all the night before. I saw them. They were zombies. They were too little to fight it off like I can. They couldn't defend themselves, so I had to defend them. I wasn't going to let her do it again. She was doing it. Going to them in their dreams and killing them. She had just murdered me in my dreams, but I woke up and I was strong and I fought it off. I had to stop her. Right then. Before she killed the children again. I had to do it. I murdered her but I had to do it."

Brunelle nodded and rubbed his chin, but didn't say anything.

"But then again," Sawyer went on, her smile returning, "you said it wasn't murder if you have to do it, right?"

Brunelle surrendered his own smile. "I did say that. If it's justified, it's not murder. Murder is an unlawful killing."

"Then I'm not guilty," Sawyer said.

Brunelle stood up. "We'll see, Ms. Sawyer. Thank you for explaining it to me."

Sawyer blinked at him, but the smile remained. "You're welcome, Mr. Brunelle. You should go home now to your girlfriend."

Chen stifled a laugh, turning it into an obviously fake cough.

"Thanks, Ms. Sawyer," Brunelle answered. "I'm sure I'll be seeing you again."

As he and Chen stepped toward the exit, Sawyer called after them. "Mr. Brunelle! If the nurse is out there, could you ask her to come in. The shot made the voices stop, but I think I'm starting to hear them again. I want to sleep, but I can't sleep very well when they talk to me."

Brunelle stared at the very earnest and very mentally ill woman strapped to the bed. "Of course, Ms. Sawyer. We'll find the nurse."

Sawyer offered a relieved smile. "Thank you, Mr. Brunelle. You're a kind man."

Brunelle shrugged. He didn't know what else to say, so he just said, "Thanks."

In the hallway, Chen finally got to tease him. "A kind man like you really should be married, you know. Should I call your girlfriend and see if she has any kids?"

Brunelle narrowed his eyes. "You know damn well my girlfriend has a kid. And if you say anything to her about us getting married I will personally dismiss every case you have with our office."

Chen laughed. "I bet I don't need to say anything."

Brunelle sighed and ran a hand over his short, gray-specked hair. "I bet you're right."

"So, at least this one isn't justified," Chen returned the conversation to work. "I doubt she was really being murdered and turned into a zombie."

Brunelle nodded. "Oh, right. No worries there. She wasn't justified."

"So the murder charge will stick?" Chen confirmed.

Brunelle shrugged. "I didn't say that. Justification isn't the only defense."

"What else are you thinking?"

"You said it," Brunelle reminded him. "She's fucking nuts. I'm staring right at an NGRI: not guilty by reason of insanity."

Chen crossed his arms. "Is she gonna walk?"

"Not if I can help it," Brunelle replied. "But I've got some work to do."

"What's the first step?" Chen asked, looking at his watch.

Brunelle looked at his too. It'd be a few hours before the medical examiner's office opened for the day.

"Breakfast," he replied. "Then I'm going to watch my girlfriend perform an autopsy."

CHAPTER 3

Dr. Kat Anderson shoved her hand up into a thick, blue, rubber glove and let it go with a loud snap.

Under different circumstances, Brunelle thought it might have been arousing. But he was there for an autopsy. Kat snapped on the other glove and Brunelle nodded approvingly.

"No mask?" His voice betrayed disappointment

Kat narrowed her eyes suspiciously and shook her head, sending her thick, black hair into a pleasant bounce. She looked great even under the scrubs. Of course, now Brunelle knew exactly how to imagine the curves beneath. "No. I need the gloves to protect me from biohazards, but I'm not too worried about spreading germs. I think she's past worrying about an infection."

"I suppose so," Brunelle responded. He found himself disappointed not to get to see her bright eyes shining out over a surgical mask. The disappointment surprised him.

I should look into that, he told himself with a small shake of his head.

"I thought the smell would be worse," he said, pulling his

thoughts away from surgical masks and hidden curves.

Kat shrugged. "She's been refrigerated. Wait 'til I cut her open."

Brunelle winced. "Great."

He'd attended one or two autopsies before, but observed through a window from an adjoining room. Usually the dead bodies he saw were fresh. The scent of blood or gunpowder could be strong, but weren't really nauseating. It took decomposition to get that truly putrid, stomach-turning stench. He steadied himself for the odor, but in doing so overlooked steeling himself for the sight.

Kat pulled back the tarp and Brunelle looked directly at what had once been Georgia Sawyer's face.

"Holy fuck!" He turned away and pressed his palms against his eyes, as if that might somehow erase the image from his mind. But the vision of the woman's former face—butchered like an inexpertly carved Thanksgiving turkey—was burned permanently into his brain.

"Wow," said Kat.

"Yeah. Wow," Brunelle agreed without turning around. "Larry said it was bad, but I had no idea."

"No," Kat said. "I mean: wow, you're a wuss."

Brunelle spun around, his manhood affronted. But he still didn't look directly at the body. "Her entire face is hacked away," he protested.

"You didn't know that?"

"Well, yeah. I knew that," Brunelle admitted. "But seeing it is different."

Kat looked down at the remains. "I don't know, David. If someone told me a person got her face hacked off with a hatchet, that's pretty much what I would expect to see."

Brunelle managed a peek at the butchered head. Exposed bone protruded from where her eye sockets and nose had once been, these fragile bone structures annihilated by the force of the hatchet blows. Her lower jaw hung open onto her throat, most of the teeth missing, and the flesh of the cheeks was slit open like the sides of a flour sack. Whatever soft tissue had once been between her brow and chin was either missing or unidentifiable. Brunelle looked away again.

"So cause of death is pretty easy, I guess," he joked darkly.

"Not much doubt there," Kat agreed with a slight grin. "But that's not where the mystery lies."

She picked up a dead wrist and examined the hand and arm. She reached over the corpse and repeated the examination for the other limb.

"No defensive wounds," she announced. "She didn't even try to fight back. So the first wound was probably fatal, or at least incapacitating. The victim likely never saw it coming."

"She was sleeping," Brunelle explained.

Kat nodded.

"Murdering children through her dreams," Brunelle explained.

Kat stopped nodding and threw a dubious glance at her boyfriend. "Excuse me?"

"Oh yeah. Her daughter explained it all to me."

"Isn't her daughter the killer?" Kat questioned.

"Yep," Brunelle confirmed. "That's how she'd know. The perfect source. She told me all about it. Her mother had been psychically murdering her in her dreams for some time. Turning her into a zombie, of course."

"Of course," Kat agreed nonchalantly.

"Which, you know, wouldn't normally be grounds for

murder," Brunelle went on, "but when mom started murdering the neighborhood kids in their dreams too, well, that went too far. She couldn't just stand by and let the little darlings be turned into zombies too."

"Oh, of course not."

"I suspect," Brunelle said, "the voices she hears when she's not doped up on intravenous anti-psychotics explained it to her much better than I'm explaining it now."

"No doubt," Kat agreed. Then she shook her head. "Wow. She's fucking nuts."

"I believe the proper term," Brunelle corrected with faux offense, "is paranoid schizophrenic."

"Probably," Kat grumbled. "I took one psych course in med school. I hated it. A bunch of gobbledygook. I like it hard, not all soft and squishy."

Brunelle smiled and rested his hand on the small of her back. "Mmm, I've noticed."

Kat had to laugh. "Wow again. Are you actually hitting on me over a dead body?"

Brunelle looked around the room appraisingly. "Why yes, I believe I am."

"That's pretty messed up, David."

He nodded. "Yeah. I should look into that."

Kat paused for a moment, then lowered her voice. "Come back tonight," she purred. "After they've cleaned the tables."

Brunelle balked at that. But he was relieved he had a limit. Probably. "Maybe just get a baby-sitter, and come over to my place?"

Kat looked up at him, locking her eyes onto his, and clanked the metal table with her knuckles. "Wuss."

CHAPTER 4

Keesha Sawyer spent another week at Harborview. It took that long to get the voices under control. She'd also nearly severed her left thumb with the hatchet.

"I needed to hold her head still once she was dead so I could keep killing her," she'd explained.

The jail didn't want her until they could be a jail and not a hospital. Once the thumb was sewn together and the voices had quieted to whispers, she was discharged into the waiting custody of two Seattle P.D. officers who drove her down James Street to the King County Jail. And once that happened, late on a Thursday night, Brunelle had twenty-four hours to file changes and arraign her. So Friday morning found him at his computer, double-checking the charging document he'd drafted days before. One count of premeditated murder in the first degree.

A knock came on his doorframe.

Brunelle looked up from his monitor. It was Nicole, one of the paralegals in the homicide unit. She'd been at the office even longer than Brunelle and knew at least as much as he did about how to prosecute a murder case. It was a shame she didn't have a law degree—if there was anyone in the office he'd want sitting next to him during a trial, it was her. Instead, she filed his witness lists and made sure his video equipment worked.

"Jessica Edwards is at the front desk," Nicole announced. "She'd like to speak with you about the Sawyer case."

"Great," Brunelle muttered as he stood up. It was anything but great, though. Edwards was one of the best at the King County Public Defender's Office. She was smart, engaging, and tenacious. Worse than that, she knew all his tricks. They'd been trying cases against each other for over a decade. The only saving grace was that he pretty much knew her tricks too. It was like experienced card players playing the hand face up on the table. They each knew what the other would do, so the only question was who got dealt the better cards.

Nicole stepped back into the hallway as Brunelle followed. "She's very pretty," Nicole added to his thoughts.

Two things struck Brunelle about Nicole's comment. First, Nicole was right. Edwards wasn't unattractive. Another asset when arguing a case in front of a jury. A subtle, unconscious one—one that shouldn't matter, but it did. Every trial attorney got a fresh haircut right before jury selection.

The second thing was that Nicole calling someone pretty was like the Sahara Desert calling something dry. Tall and buxom, with long fit legs and long brown hair, Nicole was one of those rare women who could honestly be called 'statuesque.' She was the only woman Brunelle ever thought could actually pull off a Wonder Woman costume.

Why he'd ever thought that, he wasn't sure. He'd have to look into that too.

"Sure," Brunelle agreed with a shrug, pretending he hadn't

ever noticed. "She's a good attorney too."

Edwards was waiting in the prosecutor's small reception area, thumbing through whatever old magazines some of the staff had brought in after spring cleaning.

"Jess," Brunelle greeted her as he opened the interior door to the lobby. "Nice to see you again."

Edwards set down the magazine and stood up. Nicole was right; she was attractive. Straight blond hair, cut right past the shoulder. Looked good in a suit. And pleasant features, left natural with the minimal make up she wore as a born-and-raised Northwesterner.

"Nice to see you too, Dave," she said. He knew she meant it. "You got a few minutes to talk about the Sawyer case?"

"Did you get that one?" Brunelle asked as Edwards stepped into the bowels of the prosecutor's office. "Congrats."

Edwards rolled her eyes affably. "Thanks, I think. Just once I'd like to get a case where my client didn't confess."

Brunelle smiled. "Where's the challenge in that?"

They reached his office and Edwards took a seat across the desk from him. He gestured at his computer monitor. "I just finished the charging documents."

"Murder One?" she asked.

Brunelle nodded. "Maybe we can save some time this afternoon," he joked, "if you can get the guilty plea form ready before the arraignment."

Edwards smiled, but shook her head. "Well, that's why I'm here. I think we're going to need to set over the arraignment."

Brunelle's own relaxed smile twisted into a half-frown. He knew what was coming, but he'd let himself hope it might not. The whole point of seeing each other's cards was not having to go through the song and dance of actually playing every hand. "She's competent to stand trial, Jess. She's nuts, but she's competent. Do we really need to waste time with a competency evaluation?"

Edwards shrugged, and her smile deepened. "You said it yourself, Dave. She's nuts."

Brunelle leaned back and crossed his arms. "Nuts, but not incompetent. Incompetent means she doesn't understand the proceedings against her." He started ticking off the elements on his fingertips. "Does she know she's charged with a crime? Does she know she's going to prison? Does she know I'm the bad guy trying to put her there? Does she know the pretty lady next to her is her lawyer? Does she—"

"Pretty?" Edwards interrupted. "Did you just call me pretty?"

Damn Nicole. Brunelle tried not to get flustered. "Eh, well, my point is, she may be nuts, but she knows what's going on. Can't we just skip the competency evaluation and get right to the insanity defense?"

"Insanity?" Edwards scoffed. Her smile at Brunelle's 'pretty' comment hadn't entirely faded, but she let the topic go. "I'm not going insanity."

"Why not?" Brunelle asked. He didn't miss the irony that he was advocating for a defense he likely couldn't defeat. "She totally knows what she did and why she did it. She also thinks it was justified. That's classic insanity. Not knowing right from wrong." He raised an eyebrow. "Did she tell you about the zombies?"

Edwards crossed her arms and raised an affronted chin. "What my client tells me is privileged, Mr. Brunelle." Then the chin dropped again and she smiled. "But yeah, she told me all about the zombies."

"And doesn't that sound more like insanity than incompetency?" Brunelle insisted.

"Of course it does," Edwards admitted. "But that's not the

point."

Brunelle leaned onto his desk. "What's the point then?"

"The point," Edwards explained, "is to get the best possible result for my client. And that, Dave, is not insanity."

"Insanity," Brunelle repeated. "As in '*not guilty* by reason of insanity.' When is an acquittal not the best possible result for your client?"

"When it's followed by twenty years in a mental hospital."

Brunelle didn't say anything. He just cocked his head again, inviting further explanation from his opponent.

Edwards obliged. "If she's found not guilty by reason of insanity—NGRI—then she'll automatically be committed to Western State Hospital, with a presumptive stay of twenty years, the minimum prison sentence for Murder One. Do you know how hard it is to get released after being committed for NGRI?"

"Not personally, no," Brunelle quipped. "Do you?"

Edwards groaned. "Only professionally, Dave, thank you. But getting committed with an NGRI on your file is like having 'never release' tattooed on your forehead. If they get out early and hurt somebody, the state's going to get sued ten ways 'til Sunday."

"Not my problem," Brunelle observed.

"Maybe not," Edwards agreed. "But I'm not going to set my client up for that. Not if I can help it. Tell me: what happens if they find Keesha Sawyer incompetent?"

Brunelle knew the answer. "Then they try to restore her competency."

"How?"

"With drugs."

"And if that doesn't work?"

"More drugs."

"And if those don't work?" Edwards pressed. "If they find

her unrestorable?"

Brunelle frowned. "Then we have to dismiss the charges."

Edwards crossed her arms and smiled. "See my point?"

"Not entirely. When we dismiss for incompetency, the defendant still gets committed to Western State."

"Sure, but it's a totally different situation," Edwards replied. "NGRI means a jury said you did it, but you're bat-shit crazy and don't know it's wrong to hack your mother's face off with an axe. That person isn't getting released. But if your case is dismissed because you're incompetent, that prevents any trial. There's never a judicial determination that you actually did anything."

Brunelle frowned dubiously. "Yeah, but everybody knows you did."

"Maybe," Edwards conceded, "but the doctors can hide behind that. 'She was never found guilty. She came here because she's sick. But now that we're understaffed and overbooked, we've cured her and she can be released. Yay, us.' Instead of twenty years, she'll do twenty months. Maybe."

Brunelle's expression hardened. "She murdered her mother."

Edwards offered a cynical grin. "But she's sick, Dave. I just hope the docs out at Western State can cure her quickly."

Brunelle took in what Edwards was saying. He rubbed the bridge of his nose. "So, incompetency, huh?"

Edwards shrugged a casual shoulder. "To start with. If that doesn't work, I'll try dim cap. It's even better."

"Diminished capacity?" Brunelle translated. "That means you didn't have the requisite intent to commit the crime."

"Exactly. You said yourself, she didn't know what she was doing."

"No, I said she knew exactly what she was doing, she just didn't think it was wrong."

"I dunno, Dave," Edwards grinned. "I don't think she had the intent."

"She didn't just intend it, she planned it. Jesus, she almost cut her own thumb off holding her mother's head still while she chopped some more. It couldn't have been more intentional."

Edwards' grin broadened. They both knew she was teasing. But they both knew a jury might buy what she was selling. "Well, she didn't intend to commit a *crime*. She thought it was justified."

Brunelle didn't mind a little give and take, but he was growing tired of this particular topic. Especially since it worried him. "I don't have to prove she intended to commit a crime to defeat diminished capacity," he insisted. "I have to prove that she intended to do a particular act, and that act happens to be a crime."

"Tsk, tsk." Edwards shook her head at him. "You sound like a lawyer, Dave. The jury may not understand the difference."

Brunelle surrendered a begrudging, but tight smile. "And if they get confused and find there wasn't the requisite intent—"

"Then my dim cap defense gets me an old-fashioned, no-strings-attached not guilty. Full acquittal. No jail. No hospital. Just walk out the door."

Brunelle tapped his pursed lips. "The best possible result for your client."

Edwards leaned back and crossed her legs triumphantly. "Precisely."

Brunelle glanced at the charging document still displayed on his computer screen. "I'm still going to object to a competency evaluation."

"And the judge is still going to grant it," Edwards replied confidently.

Brunelle nodded. He knew she was right. The judge was going to be very careful, allowing Edwards to explore every possible mental defense.

So much for showing his cards.

He closed his file and stood up. "Thanks for coming by, Jess. I'll see you at one o'clock."

Edwards stood up too. "I'll prepare the competency order. See you then." As Brunelle started around his desk, she waved him off. "I can find my way out."

Brunelle let her go and sat down again. The good news was that Edwards wasn't going to pursue her strongest legal defense. The bad news was that the defense she was going to pursue would lead to Keesha Sawyer being back on the streets in a matter of months.

He knew Edwards was right about that. If the case was dismissed for incompetency, they'd cut her loose as soon as they could.

They'd already done it once.

He opened the file again and looked at Keesha's criminal history.

She had a robbery charge dismissed a year earlier. 'Robbery' was a pretty strong word for her conduct. She got caught shoplifting, but when the security guard grabbed her arm, she punched him. Robbery was defined as 'using force to obtain or *retain* property.' A technical violation, and a provable one, but maybe not what was intended to be punished as a full scale robbery.

It had been her first stint in jail and she didn't deal with it well. She was hearing voices then too. The docs declared her incompetent and no one had any heartburn about dismissing a 'shoplift-gone-bad' robbery. Brunelle was cynical enough to think the psychologists might have been swayed in their competency opinion by the *de minimus* nature of the offense. So his office had dismissed the charge and six months later the hospital declared her 'cured' and released her. To the care of her mother.

"Dave?"

Brunelle looked up from the criminal history report. His boss, Matt Duncan, was standing in his doorway.

"You got a minute?" Duncan asked. As if anyone would say 'no' to the elected District Attorney.

"Of course," Brunelle replied.

"Good. There's a lawyer here I'd like you to meet. He represents the family of Georgia Sawyer. He's filing a claim against the state for Western State Hospital's early release of her daughter. I thought you might want to coordinate efforts."

Not likely, he thought. He'd dealt with enough civil attorneys to know they were a wholly different animal from criminal practitioners. If he wanted to meet with Brunelle it was just to leech off of Brunelle's efforts and use the prosecution's hard-fought conviction to obtain a hefty civil verdict with little to no work. But Brunelle pasted a smile on his face as he stood up to follow his boss to his office down the hall.

"Sounds great," he lied. "Let's go."

CHAPTER 5

The civil attorney was waiting in Duncan's office. Brunelle knew he was a civil attorney right away. First, Brunelle didn't know him, and he pretty much knew every criminal defense attorney in town. Second, he was wearing a really expensive suit. A symbol of success, but one prosecutors tended to avoid—if they could even afford it—because juries wanted their prosecutors honest, not overpaid. And third, because it was Friday. Monday through Thursday, the judges handled the criminal trials and motions and arraignments. Fridays were civil days, the one day a week the so-called 'litigation' attorneys might come to court to argue a motion to schedule a motion for a hearing about a deposition or something.

The lawyer stood up when Brunelle walked in and extended a hand in greeting. He was tall and overweight, with tanned skin and whitened teeth. He was also going bald, about right for his age, which Brunelle estimated in the mid-50s, but trying to make up for it with a thick moustache. He looked like a rich walrus.

"Pleasure to meet you, Brunelle," the walrus said, dropping the 'Mister.' Brunelle decided to take it as premature familiarity rather than disrespect. "I'm Charles Fargas," he declared. Then, as if Brunelle should know, "of Fargas and Williams."

Brunelle had never heard of the law firm, but he didn't say so. Instead, he shook Fargas' hand and said, "Nice to meet you, Mr. Fargas. Matt tells me you have an interest in one of my cases."

They separated hands and the three of them took seats around Duncan's large conference table.

"That I do," Fargas replied with a broad grin that exposed almost all of his unnaturally white teeth. "I've been retained by the family of Georgia Sawyer."

Brunelle rubbed his chin. "I thought Keesha was the family. You're not her lawyer."

It was more statement than question. Jessica Edwards was Keesha's lawyer and this guy wouldn't be caught dead, so to speak, volunteering his skills to help an indigent criminal defendant.

As if to confirm, Fargas laughed, a little too heartily. "Oh, dear Lord, no. Of course not. No, I've been retained by Georgia's sister, Louise, and her husband. They live in Oregon and weren't in regular contact, but were very distraught to hear of how the State of Washington failed to protect their loved one."

Ah, Brunelle thought. *That explains it.*

"So you're going to sue the state?" he confirmed. Then, recalling what civil law he'd been exposed to in law school, "I didn't think siblings could sue for wrongful death. Only children or dependent parents."

Fargas grinned, amused either that Brunelle knew anything at all about who could sue, or that he was naive enough to care about such alleged restrictions.

"It's not about who sues, Brunelle," he said. "It's about who you sue."

"The state," Brunelle said. "The deep pocket."

"The deepest there is." Fargas nodded. "They never should have released Keesha from her last civil commitment. If she'd still been institutionalized like she should have been, Georgia Sawyer would be alive today."

Brunelle could hardly disagree. Still, it irked him that Fargas was going to get rich from it.

"What if they don't settle?" Brunelle asked. The tone was turning from conversational to confrontational. He knew he should just let it go. He didn't. Duncan shifted in his seat.

"Oh, they'll settle," Fargas boasted.

"You better hope so," Brunelle replied. "Or you might actually have to try a case."

Fargas' confident grin withered. "I'm a litigator, Brunelle. Not just a trial attorney. There's more to litigation than just trying the case. Part of litigation is showing the other side that they better settle before trial."

Brunelle crossed his arms. "By showing them a copy of the guilty verdict I earn by actually trying the criminal case."

Fargas' smirk returned. "That will be helpful. My thanks in advance."

Duncan finally intervened before Brunelle could say any more. "Charles just wanted to let you know that he represents the surviving family and he's offered to coordinate efforts."

Brunelle nodded grimly. "Sure. I'll try the murder case. I'll prove it, beyond a reasonable doubt, despite the presumption of innocence. And after I'm done, I'll just hand you the certified court documents so you don't have to get lost trying to find the clerk's office."

Fargas narrowed his eyes over his smarmy grin. "As I said, much appreciated."

"There's only one problem," Brunelle found himself happy to

say.

Fargas' grin faded and his eyebrows knit together. "What's that?"

Brunelle's own smile replaced the civil attorney's. "Keesha Sawyer is fucking nuts. There's a very high likelihood she'll be found not guilty by reason of insanity."

Fargas shook his head firmly. "No," he barked. "That's unacceptable."

"Sorry," Brunelle said in a way that communicated quite clearly that we wasn't sorry at all. "But that may be the most just verdict. You seek the deep pocket, Fargas, but I seek justice."

Fargas sneered. "You sound like a defense attorney."

It was supposed to be an insult. Brunelle knew better. "Not at all. Defense attorneys seek an acquittal, as they should. It's the prosecutor who's responsible for finding justice."

Fargas' sneer deepened a bit, then suddenly evaporated into a well-practiced mask of false congeniality. "Well, I have faith in you, Brunelle. You'll get your justice and I'll get my settlement." He stood up and shook Duncan's hand. "I think I better be going, Matt. Thanks for setting up this meeting."

"Of course, Charles," Duncan replied as they unclasped hands. "Any time. We serve our community."

Duncan used the comment to glare at Brunelle. As they started to walk Fargas out, he turned back to Brunelle. "Stay here," he ordered.

Brunelle knew to do as he was told. A few minutes later Duncan returned from walking Fargas to the lobby and, Brunelle guessed, apologizing to the bastard.

"What the hell was that?" Duncan demanded.

Brunelle shrugged. "I don't know. He pissed me off."

"He represents the victim's family," Duncan reminded him.

"He represents himself," Brunelle countered. "He doesn't give a damn about the family. And I bet they don't give a damn about their dear sister Georgia, and her schizophrenic daughter, Keesha. Hell, that's probably why they moved to Oregon—to get the hell away from them. But now they see a big, fat payday, and Fargas gets a third."

"Don't worry about their payday," Duncan chided, "or his fee. If you meant what you said, it doesn't matter."

Brunelle thought for a moment. "Crap. What did I say?"

"You said you sought justice."

Brunelle frowned slightly, but there was a sparkle in his eye. "Damn, I hate it when I say that."

Duncan shook his head. "Fargas is well-connected, Dave. He supports the office, and me. And regardless of their motives, he does represent the victim's family. Try not to be an asshole to him."

Brunelle took a deep breath, then surrendered a begrudging nod. "Right. Sorry. I don't know what got into me."

"Just watch it next time, okay?" Duncan asked.

"Sure," Brunelle agreed. "Can I go now?"

"By all means. Go and seek justice." Duncan gestured toward his door. "But be sure to get a conviction too."

CHAPTER 6

The cameras were already in the courtroom, three of them, set up at the outer ends of the first row, aimed through the glass that separated the gallery from the secure area where the judge, lawyers, and inmates would be. Brunelle also spotted a single newspaper photographer he knew. He wasn't surprised by the media attention, but he wasn't looking for it either. He waved to them, but didn't break stride as he entered the secured section of the courtroom with a swipe of his courthouse passcard.

Edwards was waiting inside. As promised, she had the order for competency evaluation all ready.

"You wanna just agree to this?" she encouraged. "Save everybody some time?"

It was tempting. Brunelle knew the judge would almost certainly sign the order. But he also knew Keesha Sawyer was competent. "No, thanks. Let's make the judge decide."

His stance was bolstered by the fact that, in addition to the media, Brunelle had spotted Fargas in the gallery, seated with an older couple he supposed was Georgia's sister and brother-in-law. It was bad enough having cameras watching his every move; now he had a lawyer surveilling him too. A lawyer who liked suing people, especially people who worked for government agencies. A lawyer Brunelle had pissed off. Better put on a show.

"Suit yourself." Edwards shrugged. Then she looked up at the stack of files on the bar in front of the judicial clerk. "Can you get us on first?"

The courtroom was officially called 'Presiding.' It was where all of the day-to-day, meat-grinding, sausage-making of criminal law took place. All afternoon, every afternoon, was nothing but arraignment after arraignment. The only plea allowed was 'not guilty.' Guilty pleas take twenty minutes, the judge having to go over a ten-page form and every constitutional right the defendant was giving up by pleading guilty. If you wanted to plead guilty, first you pled *not guilty*, so they could get to the one hundred other cases docketed that afternoon. Then, you could schedule a plea hearing—which was what Presiding did all morning while the prosecutors were upstairs reviewing last night's police reports for the afternoon arraignments. Plea after plea, all morning, every morning.

Justice, or a reasonable facsimile thereof.

It was an efficient way to deal with the ninety-five percent of criminal cases that resolved through plea-bargaining. But it was mind-numbingly repetitive. The judges rotated in and out of Presiding every six months, enduring the ordeal only because of the promise of not having to do it again for several years as the other judges each took their own turn. Similarly, the prosecutor's and public defender's offices each assigned a younger attorney to spend all day, every day, putting the cases on the record. It wasn't a plum assignment, but it was the first step into felony court, and most of them were happy enough to be moving on with their careers, leaving behind the shoplifting and driving while suspended cases.

The best part for one of these Young Turks was when a big case hit the docket and the actual trial attorneys came down to handle it. That meant they could step aside for a few minutes and relax a bit from the relentless onslaught of charge and conviction.

"Hello, Mr. Brunelle," said the young prosecutor as he lined up his files for the afternoon. Brunelle was pretty sure his name was Brad. Or Bill. Probably Brad. "Are you handling a matter yourself?"

Brunelle had kind of liked it at first when other prosecutors starting calling him 'Mr. Brunelle.' It showed respect and he wasn't that old yet. Then, when he crossed forty, it started to bug him for a while because he had become, after all, that old. Now, a few years later, temples flecked with gray and a file cabinet full of high-profile murder cases, he mostly ignored it.

"Yeah," he confirmed. "The Sawyer arraignment. Any chance I could go first?"

Brad may have been junior to Brunelle, but it was still his calendar to run. He knew how many cases there were, who was in custody and who wasn't, what the charges were, who had already hired a private attorney and who was going to get stuck with the public defender standing at the opposite end of the bar.

Brunelle looked over to see if he knew the public defender. The answer was definitely no. He would have remembered her. He barely noticed Brad's response of, "Of course, Mr. Brunelle," as he took in the woman standing just a few feet away from him.

Tall, thin, reddish-brown curls hanging to her jaw line, bright blue eyes. And young. Not quite young enough to be his daughter, but young enough that a few years earlier he could have been arrested for doing what he was thinking just then.

She noticed him looking at her. She turned and smiled, producing a perfect dimple in her right cheek. "Hello, Mr. Brunelle."

She knew his name.

"Uh, hi," he stammered. Then he straightened up a bit and tried to exude the confidence which ought to have been associated with everyone calling him 'Mr. Brunelle.' "Are you handling the Sawyer case too?"

It was a lame question. Edwards was sitting right there at one of the lawyer tables.

"Of course not, Dave," Edwards stood up and smacked Brunelle amicably in the chest with her proposed order. "Robyn just started in here. I'm not going to do that to her."

Brunelle noticed Edwards was the only one in the room who didn't call him 'Mr. Brunelle.' It just showed they were friends as well as opponents. "Right. Of course. Dumb question, I guess. I thought maybe you'd let her get some experience."

Robyn smiled—that dimple again—and winked at Brunelle. "I'm pretty experienced."

Brunelle felt a blush rise out of his collar, so he nodded and turned quickly to his file which he opened to no particular place. After a moment, he remembered to extract the charging documents. "Here you go." He handed copies to Edwards without looking up from his file.

Mercifully, the judge entered and the bailiff called out, "All rise!"

Brunelle was relieved to have his awkwardness with Robyn terminated by outside stimuli. He was less relieved when he saw who the judge was. Michael Adams. One of the new ones. Just elected the past fall. He'd even grown a full beard since then to try to look more judicial, but it just highlighted the complete lack of hair on top of his head.

There was no way a new judge would have the guts to deny a defense request for a competency evaluation. Denying it was an automatic issue on appeal. Not necessarily a losing issue, but an issue nonetheless. It took an experienced judge to feel confident enough to take a chance of doing something the appellate courts wouldn't like. Experience being right in the face of a challenge, and experience not caring about being labeled wrong by a bunch of Monday-morning quarterbacks in black robes.

The last thing a new judge wanted was to be overturned on appeal. Actually, the last thing a new judge wanted was to draw an opponent in the next election, and one way to draw an opponent was to be seen as vulnerable because he keeps getting overturned on appeal.

Brunelle announced the case and prepared for his quixotic attempt to block the competency evaluation and its attendant delay of his prosecution. He knew he'd lose, but he'd put on a show. After all, there were cameras. And Fargas. And Robyn.

"The first matter that's ready is the State of Washington versus Keesha Sawyer," he said as the jailers brought Sawyer in from a secure door to the holding cells behind the courtroom. "I'm handing forward to the court copies of the charging documents and ask that we proceed to arraignment."

Judge Adams took the offered papers from his clerk and looked down at Edwards. "Is the defense ready to do the arraignment?"

"Absolutely not, Your Honor," Edwards seemed almost proud to say. "My client is not competent to stand trial, let alone be arraigned."

That sent the appropriate murmur through the gallery. Brunelle tried to remember whether he'd mentioned the competency issue to Fargas.

Judge Adams also seemed impressed. Or scared.

"Oh. Well. Um," he stammered. Prior to being elected,

Adams had been a family law attorney. He did divorces, child custody disputes, etc., so he knew his way around a courtroom well enough, but we wasn't very well versed in criminal law yet. "So what do we do now?"

At least he was honest about it. Every judge is new at some point, and every judge has areas of the law he or she never really practiced. You could tell the judges who were going to be good because they didn't hide their ignorance behind their black robes. They admitted it and sought input from the advocates. The ones who blustered and belittled to distract from their own ignorance, those were the ones lawyers hated going in front of.

"Well," Edwards started, "if you're willing to take my word for it, you could just dismiss the charges now. Otherwise, my client needs to undergo a psychiatric evaluation."

Adams looked to Brunelle for confirmation.

Brunelle didn't provide it. "The State disagrees that there's any reason to doubt Ms. Sawyer's competency," he began. "Admittedly, she has mental health issues, but she appears perfectly capable of understanding the situation she finds herself in now. Her mental issues touch more on the State's ability to prove the charges, rather than the State's ability to proceed with the prosecution."

"If I might, Your Honor?" Edwards interrupted. "It's not Mr. Brunelle who should be deciding whether my client is competent. We have psychologists at Western State Hospital who do that."

Again the judge looked to Brunelle. The indecision was clear on his face. Maybe Brunelle actually had a chance after all.

"I would submit, Your Honor," he said, "that we don't need to go to that waste of time and expense. The defense is moving the court for an evaluation. You can deny that motion if you see no reason to doubt her competency. The core question is whether she understands the charges against her and the nature of the proceedings. You could simply inquire of her, right here in open court, whether she knows what she's charged with, why, and what could happen if she's convicted. Ask her who you are, who I am, who Ms. Edwards is. Ask her what a trial is for and what witnesses do. Based on my experience with the case, I believe she will answer all those questions in a way that will satisfy the court that she's competent to stand trial."

Adams looked to Edwards. "Any objection to that, Ms. Edwards?"

Edwards scowled and crossed her arms. "Absolutely, Your Honor." She glared at Brunelle for a moment, clearly irritated that the judge was even considering denying her motion. "First of all, my client has a right to remain silent. You can't compel her to answer those questions. More importantly—and with all due respect, Your Honor—you're not a psychologist. You have no specialized training in this field. Even if Ms. Sawyer could parrot back the right answers, that doesn't mean she's competent. Let the experts handle this. If they say she's competent, then we can arraign her. There's no reason to rush this. She's not going anywhere."

Brunelle frowned slightly. That was a good point. There was no rush. And while she was at Western State, she would be held without any right to post bail. She wasn't going anywhere.

Adams looked to Brunelle one last time, but Brunelle was out of bullets. "She's competent, Your Honor," he insisted. "This is a waste of time."

The judge nodded for several seconds. He rubbed his chin. He pursed his lips. He stroked his new beard a few times. By the time he'd finished the tics, Brunelle was pretty sure he'd lost.

"I understand Mr. Brunelle's concerns about conserving judicial resources and not delaying matters unduly," he began. Brunelle knew it was bad to be mentioned first because that meant he'd be followed by the inevitable 'but.' "But it seems to me that there is no prejudice to either side to wait the short amount of time it will take the doctors at Western State Hospital to evaluate Ms. Sawyer. Whereas, if I deny the request for an evaluation, there may be great prejudice to Ms. Edwards and the defendant."

Which would result in a reversal on appeal, Brunelle finished in his head.

"I will grant Ms. Edwards' motion for a competency evaluation and we will set the matter for a hearing in two weeks to find out the results of the evaluation."

Edwards thanked the judge and handed her order to the clerk. Adams signed it and within moments, Keesha Sawyer was being escorted back into the bowels of the jail, her fate having been determined by people who barely even acknowledged her presence before them. Brunelle and Edwards each gathered their things up and Brad went ahead and called the next case.

"Satisfied now?" Brunelle asked Edwards amicably.

"Nope," she replied with a smile. "That was step one. Step two is making sure the docs say she's incompetent."

"You're going to coach your client on how to game the eval?"

"David! I am hurt you would even suggest that." But her grin belied her assertion. "It's simply that she has the right to have her lawyer present during the evaluation, so I will be sure to direct the attention of the doctors to the information most relevant for their determination."

"Most relevant to help you," Brunelle translated. "And nothing that helps me."

The small talk wasn't just the usual post-hearing banter among attorneys. Brunelle was waiting for Fargas to leave, and relaxed a bit when he watched him finally exit the gallery with his clients.

"Okay, then," Brunelle said, wrapping it up. "You win round one, but this is just the beginning."

"You have not yet begun to litigate," Edwards joked. "Or something like that."

"Something liked that," Brunelle confirmed with a smile.

He stole one last glance at Robyn New-Lawyer, her red curls swaying slightly as she spoke to the judge. She seemed to sense it, as she turned around and gave him one last dimpled smile. Brunelle managed to smile back, then hurried through the security door and out into the hallway. He had known he was going to lose that hearing, but he still didn't like it. Either way, though, it was over. He could head up to his office to consider his next steps in some peace and quiet.

"Brunelle!" came a shout from behind him. He turned to see Fargas storming at him, flanked by his clients. "You have some explaining to do!"

CHAPTER 7

"What just happened in there?" Fargas demanded.

His clients stood to the side and slightly behind him, a couple in their fifties, nicely dressed. The woman offered an awkward, apologetic smile. The man's face was grim, his arms crossed. Brunelle looked back to their lawyer.

"She was ordered out to Western State for a competency evaluation," Brunelle answered.

"I know that," Fargas blustered. "We were in the damn gallery. What I want to know is why. And why you didn't say anything about it before."

Ah, Brunelle realized. Fargas had forgotten to tell his clients about this possibility. So he looked stupid, or at least unprepared. Maybe both.

"I would have thought," Brunelle enjoyed saying, "that you would have foreseen this eventuality, given the nature of your claim against the state."

Fargas' eyes twitched at the jab, but it worked. Mrs. Client's slight smile at Brunelle turned into a clear frown at Fargas. Mr.

Client's grim glare didn't change, but did transfer from Brunelle to Fargas.

Now the overture to Fargas' clients. "I do apologize," Brunelle said. "I should have mentioned it. I knew it was coming and although I argued against it, I anticipated the judge would grant it. I'm confident she'll be found competent, though, and then we can proceed with the prosecution."

Then he addressed Fargas' clients directly. "If there's anything I or my office can do for you, please don't hesitate to ask."

Mrs. Client smiled. "Thank you, Mr. Brunelle."

Her husband just nodded curtly.

"I'm their attorney, Brunelle," Fargas reminded him. "Your office can go through me."

Brunelle didn't say anything. He knew Fargas was right, and besides his goal hadn't been to connect with the clients as much as to disrupt their connection with Fargas. The last thing he needed was hostile family.

For his part, Fargas finally showed some judgment: he ended the conversation. He jabbed a finger at Brunelle. "Keep me informed."

Brunelle forced a smile and nodded. "Will do, Charles."

Fargas gestured to his clients to follow him and stormed by Brunelle. Georgia's sister reached out and touched Brunelle's arm as she passed. "Thank you again."

Brunelle smiled, for real this time. "You're welcome."

It was nice to feel appreciated.

CHAPTER 8

The clinking of dishes and the sizzle of woks mixed genially with the growing conversations as the crowds started to thicken at The Jade House, the Chinese restaurant that was starting to become Brunelle and Kat's regular dinner spot. At least on Fridays.

"And then he said," Brunelle went on, punctuating his point with a jab of his fork, "'Keep me informed'."

Kat nodded and raised her own chopsticks to her mouth. Cashew chicken. "Oh yeah?"

"Yeah," Brunelle affirmed. "So I said, 'Will do, Charles'. He was just so aggressive. I get along fine with the defense attorneys. I don't know why the civil attorneys think they're supposed to be jerks all the time."

Kat gave a crooked smile as she chewed. "We deal a lot more with you criminal types," she said, "but every now and again one of those corporate suit lawyers will call and ask us to do something for them."

"Like what?" Brunelle mumbled through his basil beef.

"Well, about a month ago," Kat related, "we had a suspicious death. No external violence to the body, but no known illnesses either. And she was young. Thirty-something. But just as we're ready to crack her open, we get a call from some big law firm downtown. The husband's hired a lawyer and they're trying to block the autopsy on religious grounds."

Brunelle raised an eyebrow. "Sounds suspicious."

Kat nodded. "I thought so too. I mean, the husband? That's always the first suspect."

Brunelle laughed. He smiled at his girlfriend. "Absolutely."

"On the other hand," Kat continued, "he's also the one who would know about any religious objections and care enough to try to stop it."

Brunelle nodded. "Fair enough. So what did you do?"

Kat chuckled. "I don't even remember. My boss handled it. I just remember the lawyer was a complete dick."

Brunelle laughed and took another bite. The noise in the restaurant was picking up. It threatened to drown out the conversation at their usual table that was almost but not quite too close to the kitchen.

"Yeah, well this guy is definitely a complete dick too," Brunelle said. "I just hope he stays out of my way." He thought for a minute. "If I can even get going on my way, that is. We couldn't even do the arraignment. She got sent out to Western State for a competency eval."

It was Kat's turn to nod. "Well, you said she was crazy," she reminded him before popping another bite in her mouth.

"Sure, but she's not incompetent," Brunelle replied. He didn't want to explain it again. Instead, he was about to tell her the timetable for getting the evaluation competed and the case back on track. But she beat him to the next comment.

"I'm just glad they're already dead before I get into their

heads. Brains are a lot simpler when they're just wrinkled gray flesh."

Brunelle grimaced and looked down at his beef. It was more of a brown than gray, but still. "Yeah, well, anyway, the eval should be done within two weeks. Then we can arraign her and get this thing moving again."

Kat washed down her next bite with a sip of wine. "I always wondered about those guys in med school who wanted to become psychiatrists. They always seemed to be pretty screwed up themselves."

"Maybe they just wanted to understand themselves better," Brunelle suggested with a grin. "Doctors are notorious narcissists."

Kat raised an eyebrow. "Excuse me? Doctors? What about lawyers?"

Brunelle raised his own eyebrows. He drew himself up in his seat. "I serve the public, madam."

Kat laughed out loud. "Oh please. You serve yourself, Mr. Brunelle. Not that I'm complaining. I like a confident man, but you're as much a narcissist as any doctor."

Brunelle felt a little stung by the comment. His expression must have shown it as he searched for a reply.

"Come on, David." She smiled beneath narrowing eyes and pointed her chopsticks at him. "Three times just now I tried to comment about my work or my experiences, and three times you steered the conversation right back to *you* and *your* case."

Brunelle's eyebrows knitted. He wasn't sure that was true. And even if it was, hadn't she done the same thing? Wasn't that how a conversation worked?

"I'm sorry," he offered anyway. "I didn't realize."

"Of course you didn't," she teased. "That's because you're a narcissist."

Brunelle smiled at the barb, but only to cover the twinge in his gut.

"You should look into that," Kat jabbed again over her wine glass.

Brunelle's smile weakened. "Yeah," he decided to agree as he pushed at what was left of his beef and rice. "Maybe so."

CHAPTER 9

The competency hearing was scheduled for two weeks after the aborted arraignment, so of course the evaluation report showed up on Day 13. In the afternoon.

Nicole walked into Brunelle's office and handed him the multi-page fax.

"Who uses a fax machine anymore?" he asked as he took the document. "It's positively medieval."

Nicole smiled. "Well, it is a mental institution," she said. "There's something inherently medieval about that."

"I suppose so," Brunelle agreed. He was no student of history, but he had a mental image of a medieval asylum—and it looked like Hell on Earth. He fought off a shudder and tapped the front of the report. "Did you read it?"

Nicole put a fist on her hip and cocked her head. "Well, of course."

Whenever she did something like that with her body, it just reminded Brunelle how much poise and grace was packed into that statuesque frame. He didn't know much about her personal life. She wasn't one to talk about it; he wasn't one to ask. But she held herself like someone who'd stared down some pretty tough demons and come out the stronger for it.

"What does it say?" His question wasn't spurred by laziness. He'd read the report full through. It was just that the reports were written almost as crazy as the people they were about. One would expect the reports to start with the answer everyone cared about: is the defendant competent? Brunelle would have liked a large "Yes" or "No" at the top, maybe with check boxes next to them. But instead, the reports were typically twelve or fourteen pages, reciting all of the defendant's criminal history and childhood tragedies, followed by a detailed description of his or her current grooming and hygiene habits. Finally, somewhere toward the end, but not the very end—that would be too easy to find—buried in the middle of some paragraph, would be one ambiguous sentence, neither boldfaced nor italicized, that said something like, 'The patient presents as understanding the nature of the charges against her, however there may be some question as to whether her paranoid delusions might impair her ability to effectively assist her counsel.'

Sometimes he thought the doctors were as crazy as the patients.

"It says she's competent," Nicole reported.

He exhaled. Thank God. He'd been worried. They'd found her incompetent once before, although he was still convinced that was because the doctors felt sorry for her and didn't want her prosecuted for shoplifting food. But this was murder. The shrinks needed to get out of his way. He was glad they had.

"Barely competent," Nicole clarified. "And only because she's been on intravenous anti-psychotics since the night of the murder."

Brunelle slapped the report onto his desk and displayed an exaggerated grin. "Good enough for me!"

He considered reading the entire report just then, but then he remembered the hour. The courthouse would be closing in ninety minutes. "I wonder where Jessica is right now."

Western State had certainly faxed the report to her too, but the public defender's office was notorious for letting faxes and voicemails back up. Hundreds of needy clients who get your services for free can clog up an in-box pretty fast.

Nicole smiled. That smile of satisfaction she always wore when she knew her attorneys as well as they knew themselves. Maybe even better. "I already checked. She has three pretrials this afternoon, all in the Pit."

Brunelle nodded and stood up, pulling the report from his desk. "Thanks, I bet I can catch her."

Nicole stepped almost enough out of Brunelle's way as he passed. "I already made a copy for her. It's on my desk."

Brunelle turned back from his door frame. "Thanks, Nicole. You're the best."

She curtsied—like an Amazon princess, Brunelle thought. "I know."

CHAPTER 10

The Pit was to pretrial conferences what Presiding was to arraignments and pleas. After all, arraignments had to turn into pleas somehow, and somewhere. The somehow was plea-bargaining, and the somewhere was pretrials in the Pit, semi-formal court dates scheduled to make sure the busy prosecutors and overworked defense attorneys would actually get together to discuss their cases. A defense attorney might stack up five of six pretrials on the same date, each with a different prosecutor. But that was okay because each of those prosecutors had seven or eight pretrials, each with a different defense attorney. In fact, the prosecutor's property crimes unit had so many cases, they had a prosecutor assigned to do nothing but negotiate cases all day. The drug unit had two. So everyone showed up in the Pit, a large room next door to Presiding where criminal cases were wheeled and dealed like the trading pit of a stock exchange.

Brunelle found Edwards at the far end, in a heated conversation with a prosecutor from the Special Assault Unit.

"It was a party," Edwards was insisting. "My guy was drunk.

So was she."

"She was fourteen," the prosecutor replied. An implacable woman in a dark suit. Brunelle had worked with her before; she was tough.

"Fourteen-year-olds get drunk," Edwards tried.

"They get raped too," the prosecutor replied. "No deals. He pleads as charged or we go to trial."

Edwards was about to pretend that she didn't mind going to trial on a child rape case where her main defense appeared to be that the victim kind of deserved it. Brunelle saved her from that.

"Jess, you got a minute?" He raised the document in his hand. "We just got the eval on Sawyer."

Edwards seemed relieved to disengage from her negotiations. But they all knew she'd be back in a few minutes, ready with some new angle she'd claim merited a reduction in the charges.

"The eval, huh?" She snatched it out of Brunelle's hand. "It better say she's incompetent."

Brunelle grinned. "You think I'd come all the way down here to find you if it did?"

Edwards looked up from her reading of the report long enough to shoot Brunelle a glare. Then she went back to flipping roughly through the pages. "Where is it? Where is the damn conclusion? Argh. Why do they write these like this?"

"I think it's because the doctors are crazy too," Brunelle quipped. It was easy to be light-hearted when he'd won the competency battle.

Edwards didn't seem to appreciate it.

"They said she was incompetent before," she argued to no one in particular as she finally settled in on the last page and began reading. "Why would they say she's competent now?"

"Probably because before, she stole a pack of cigarettes, and this time she murdered her mother."

"It was some grapes," Edwards corrected without looking up. "She was hungry."

"Even better," Brunelle said.

Edwards allowed a smirk. "Mr. Brunelle, are you suggesting that the doctors at Western State Hospital allow their competency determinations be influenced by their personal feeling about the appropriateness of a particular prosecution?"

Brunelle shrugged. "If the straitjacket fits."

Edwards shook her head. "They wouldn't do that. They're professionals. Like us."

"I don't know," Brunelle chuckled. "I was told recently that lawyers are all narcissists."

Edwards looked up. "Who told you that?"

"A doctor, actually," Brunelle realized. "A medical examiner."

"Oh," Edwards looked back down at the report. "You mean the one you're fucking?"

Brunelle's jaw dropped. He wasn't sure what bothered him more: that people knew about his relationship, or the vulgarity Edwards just used to express it.

"Wow," he sputtered. "You're in a mood."

Edwards glowered at him. "Don't tell me what kind of mood to be in."

Before Brunelle could reply, the young defense attorney from Presiding stepped over. Robyn. "Whoa," she said. "Tense."

Edwards glared at her too, but Brunelle offered a bemused smile.

"So," Robyn said conversationally, holding the word long enough to indicate she was about to try to lighten the mood. "Who are you fucking?"

Brunelle was mortified, but Edwards let out a huge laugh. When she saw Brunelle's expression, she laughed even harder.

"The medical examiner," Edwards said at last, gasping. "He's fucking the medical examiner."

"Ooh." Robyn nodded and twirled some of her red curls with an absent finger. "Kinky."

Brunelle shook his head and raised his palms in protest. "No, it's not like that."

"It isn't?" Robyn let a pout play across her red lips. "That's too bad."

Brunelle cocked his head at the pretty young lawyer. His smile started to return, but before he could figure out anything to say, Edwards shook the report at him. "This is bullshit, Dave, and you know it."

"I know it's *not* bullshit," he replied. "Remember, I spoke with her in the hospital. She gets what she did and what she's facing. She just thinks it was okay."

"Wait," Robyn interrupted. "You interrogated the defendant yourself and you're fucking the coroner? Sounds like some serious conflicts of interest."

Brunelle wasn't interested in having two arguments at once. He was about to say something rude, when Robyn beat him to the punch. "No worries, though. I like a dirty prosecutor." Then she turned to Edwards. "Can I see the report?"

Edwards handed it to her and she began flipping through it as Edwards and Brunelle argued.

"You're not a psychologist, Dave," Edwards started.

"Neither are you. And the psychologists say she's competent."

"They say that this time, but only because they're afraid of getting sued."

"Can you blame them? The last time they let her out, somebody's face ended up all over a wall."

"Which just proves she's crazy."

"She may be crazy, but she's not incompetent."

"How can she be competent if she's crazy?"

Brunelle ran his hands through his hair. They were getting nowhere and he didn't want to have the same argument yet again. "Can we just set the arraignment and get this thing moving?"

"What's the rush, Mr. B.?" Robyn suddenly interjected. She handed the report back to Edwards. "We don't have to accept this. We can get an independent evaluation and fight it out at a contested competency hearing."

Edwards and Brunelle both stared at her for a moment. She was right. The statutes provided for an independent defense evaluation, but there was an unspoken gentleman's—or gentleperson's—agreement between the prosecutor's office and the defense bar to accept the opinions of the doctors at Western State. Their office had done that when they'd found Sawyer incompetent on the grapes case, dismissing it when Western State said she was incompetent. Brunelle expected Edwards to do the reverse now: bitch about the report, but accept it and let the prosecution move forward.

But Edwards' grin told him she wouldn't be doing that after all. "Excellent idea, Miss Dunn."

Now wait a minute," Brunelle started to protest, but it was too late.

"Any ideas for who we should hire to do our evaluation?" Edwards asked her, ignoring Brunelle.

"As a matter of fact, yes," Robyn replied with a broad smile. Brunelle didn't like that dimple so much any more. "I happen to know a very qualified psychologist. He's a good friend, and the director of Cascade Mental Hospital."

Brunelle's eyebrows shot up. Cascade Mental Hospital was a private mental hospital on the Eastside—the suburbs on the other side of Lake Washington from Seattle. It had started out as an exclusive sanatorium offering spa services and electroshock therapy to a clientele of successful businessmen. However, as the field of psychology progressed and it became less socially acceptable to commit 'nervous' wives and 'defective' children, the facility fell into disrepair. It was barely holding on as an emergency spill-over facility when the state-run mental institutions became overcrowded.

"That dump?" Brunelle scoffed. "I didn't know they even had real psychologists."

"Oh, it's very real out there," Robyn assured with a glint in her eye.

Brunelle crossed his arms. "How do you know they'll say what you want?"

Robyn batted her eyelashes and her lips curled into a smile simultaneously innocent and anything but. "I can be very convincing."

Brunelle had no doubt about that.

CHAPTER 11

"No fucking way."

That's what Chen had said when Brunelle asked the detective to accompany him to Cascade Mental Hospital.

"That's not in Seattle," Chen was quick to point, "so it's out of my jurisdiction. Sorry, pal."

Brunelle knew it was bullshit. "You scared of that place, Larry?"

"I'll tell you, Dave," the detective explained. "I used to have to drive some of the crazy-birds out there when I was still doing patrol. That place was creepy as hell then and I've heard it's only gotten worse. I wouldn't say I'm scared of it exactly, but I know this: after you've been there, you'll be scared too."

The conversation had felt like a challenge at the time, but as Brunelle drove up the long drive to the crumbling facade of the asylum, he reassessed it from challenging to prophetic.

Cascade was, in fact, creepy as hell. It looked like a cross between an old English manor house and a 1950s public school. It was a large, sprawling building, finished in orange brick and gray stone, with gables and turrets that decorated a roof looming heavily over three floors of iron-barred windows.

Brunelle fought off a shiver and parked his car in the gravel lot near the front door. It was a bright day and the heat from the sun bounced off the dusty ground as he stepped from his car and looked up again at the facility. He reminded himself that it was a hospital—a mental hospital, but still a hospital. There needed to be a place to house people unable to care for themselves. Western State couldn't take everyone. Cascade served an important community function, he told himself. Just like the prosecutor's office.

Brunelle straightened his tie and walked toward the entrance, intent on his mission to remind the director of their shared goal of public safety, hopefully before Edwards contacted him for her 'independent' evaluation. Edwards could try to game the system, but Brunelle knew how to play the game too. A phone call would have been too easy to disregard, or not even take. He was going to look the doctor in the eye, shake his hand, and get a commitment from him to give the *right* answer, not just the answer Edwards and Robyn wanted.

Brunelle pulled open the heavy wooden front door and stepped inside. Despite the rows of windows he'd seen from the outside, the lobby was devoid of sunlight, starkly dark in contrast to the sunny day outside. Hallways led off the lobby to his left, right, and straight ahead. At the back of the lobby was a large wooden reception desk, but it was empty. The only person he could see was a very large man in a hospital gown sitting on a bench about halfway down the long hallway to his left. The man had wild, unruly hair and, if Brunelle was seeing it correctly, an eye patch. There were no staff members to be seen anywhere, but the large man didn't seem to care. He was sitting as still as a statue, his only movement a barely perceptible rocking front to back.

Brunelle walked up to the reception desk, hoping maybe the receptionist was simply out of sight, perhaps picking something up off the floor or asleep with their head on the desk. No such luck, however. He was definitely alone in the foyer. A hotel style bell sat on the desk with a handwritten sign that read, 'Ring Once.'

Brunelle looked around. What other choice did he have?

Ding!

The large man jumped to his feet and began yelling something at once unintelligible and angry. A nurse suddenly appeared from the center hallway and ran over to the large man, glaring at Brunelle as she raced past.

"It's okay, Eddie. It's okay." She grabbed the large man by his thick arms and looked up at him. He was at least a foot taller than her and was looking up at the ceiling, moaning. "He didn't know, Eddie. The bad man didn't know. It's okay. The bells are gone now. The bells are bye-bye. It's okay."

After a few more minutes of similar soothing and promises of the bell being 'bye-bye', One-Eyed Eddie calmed down enough for the nurse to ease him back onto the bench. She lingered a moment as Eddie settled back into his catatonic rocking, then she marched directly toward Brunelle, hands balled into fists, jaw clenched in anger.

"Just what do you think you're doing?" she demanded.

Brunelle tapped the 'Ring Once' sign. He wasn't sure whether he should be indignant for being asked, scared by Eddie's reaction, or thankful for the nurse coming to his rescue. He settled for feeling generally freaked out. "It says to ring the bell," he defended.

"*Not*," the nurse crossed her arms, "when Eddie is in the hallway."

Brunelle glanced again at the sign. Indignancy was making a

comeback. "Yeah, it doesn't say that."

The nurse flared her nostrils and growled slightly. She was an unpleasant looking woman. She had stringy black hair pulled back into a ponytail, with dirty looking bangs hanging too far over her baggy eyes and putty nose. "What do you want, Mr.—?"

"Brunelle. Dave Brunelle. I'm with the King County Prosecutor's Office."

Brunelle had to admit, he sometimes enjoyed the reaction he got from saying that. Cocktail party conversation to be sure, but this was one of those times too. The baggy eyes widened and she reflexively wiped her hands on her skirt. "Prosecutor's office? Why? Is this about—?" But she stopped herself.

Brunelle raised an eyebrow, curious, but willing to see what she said next.

Unfortunately, the nurse calmed herself. The darkness returned to her eyes and she set her mouth into a grim line. "What can I help you with, Mr. Brunelle?"

Brunelle offered his own fake expression: a smile. "I was wondering if I could speak with Dr. Adrianos." He decided not to elaborate on why he wanted to speak with the hospital's director, even if just because it was fun to play with Nurse Baggy-Eyes.

For her part, the nurse wasn't completely oblivious to Brunelle's coyness. She worked in a mental hospital after all. She shifted her weight, then crossed her arms again and nodded. "Dr. Adrianos is a very busy man. Do you have an appointment?"

Brunelle kept his saccharine grin. "I'm afraid not, but I'm willing to wait. It won't take long, I promise."

The nurse sneered at the word 'promise.' Brunelle had noticed that to be a common female reaction to the word. "Can I tell him what it's regarding?"

Brunelle let the smile slip away, replacing it with his 'serious and professional' expression. "Murder," he said a bit too dramatically. "It's about murder."

The nurse narrowed her eyes, but didn't say anything for a moment. Then she pointed at his feet. "Stay here," she commanded, then disappeared down the long hallway she'd emerged from.

Brunelle was willing to remain in the lobby, but he wasn't about to be ordered to stand in one spot. He turned, clasped his hands behind his back, and began a slow stroll around the tiled foyer.

One-Eyed Eddie was still rocking glacially on his bench. There was a distant, barely audible sound of screaming from somewhere down the other hallway. And directly in front of him was the door to the outside. He resisted the urge to run to his car and flee.

"Mr. Brunelle!" boomed a voice behind him.

Brunelle turned to see a large man, younger than him, with thick golden curls, a blond goatee, and a brilliant smile charging right toward him. He stuck out a meaty hand in greeting. "I'm Peter Adrianos. I've been expecting you."

CHAPTER 12

"You've been expecting me?" Brunelle asked dumbly as he shook Adrianos' hand.

"Of course!" Adrianos laughed. "You're a lawyer. Everyone knows lawyers are all crazy. It was only a matter of time until you ended up here."

"Ah." Brunelle managed a smile as he extracted his hand. "Got it. Good one."

The psychologist reached out and clasped Brunelle on the shoulder. He had a strong grip. "Seriously though, Robyn already called me. She told me all about poor Keesha. I knew I'd hear from you eventually, although I expected a phone call. To what do I owe the honor of this in-person visit?"

Brunelle hadn't overlooked the 'poor Keesha' comment. He was probably already too late. Still, he'd come this far, and he hadn't been completely unprepared for the possibility that the defense attorneys would have reached out to Adrianos first.

"I think I may need a primer on competency versus insanity," Brunelle said. He knew the difference just fine, thank you, but Adrianos seemed like someone who thought pretty highly of himself. Brunelle decided to play to his vanity. "I thought you might be willing to take the time to educate me. Robyn spoke very highly of you and, in all honesty, I just don't see how she and Jessica can be so convinced Keesha is incompetent. Either they're lying or I'm wrong. And I thought that kind of conversation would be more productive in person."

Adrianos listened intently, nodding and mm-hmming at all the appropriate places.

"Yes, yes, I quite agree," he said. "Robyn said you were an honest prosecutor. Well, Robyn didn't say that. She said you were dashing and experienced. But she said Jessica said you were honest. I can see that as well. Come back to my office and let's discuss mental illness, shall we?"

He took Brunelle by the elbow—much to the chagrin of Nurse Angry—and steered him into the bowels of Cascade Mental Hospital. The nurse huffed, and One-Eyed Eddie was moaning slightly, but Brunelle hardly noticed. His mind was filled with a different noise:

'Robyn said you were dashing.'

* * *

Adrianos' office was immense, of course. A wall of windows looked out onto an enclosed courtyard dotted with patients and staff. One nurse was pushing a patient in a wheelchair. Two other nurses were taking a cigarette break under a tree. Several patients were just walking around aimlessly. One patient was exposing himself to some flowers, and appeared pleased by their reaction.

"So," Adrianos practically shouted as he sat down behind his massive oaken desk. "Competency to stand trial. Quite the problematic mystery, eh, counselor?"

Brunelle sat back in his leather guest chair opposite

Adrianos. "Well, I'm not so sure it's problematic or mysterious. In fact, it seems pretty straightforward to me. Does a person understand the charges against him and the nature of the court proceedings? Keesha sure seems to know she's being prosecuted for murder."

"But she thinks it was justified," Adrianos pointed out.

"Which means she's insane," Brunelle replied, "not incompetent. In fact, I'd say the fact that she believes it was justified in her particular case shows that she knows, generally speaking, murder is wrong."

Adrianos shook his head and steepled his hands at the fingertips. "But don't you see? It's precisely that sort of fixed delusion that makes her incompetent."

Brunelle didn't see. He said as much.

"That's because," Adrianos continued, in a voice both pedagogic and patronizing, "you've forgotten about the other part of incompetency. A person is incompetent to stand trial if they suffer from a mental defect that prevents them from *either* understanding the charges and proceedings against them *or* from assisting their attorney in the presentation of their defense. Keesha's fixed delusions of justification prevent her from assisting Jessica and Robyn."

"First of all," Brunelle raised a finger, "Robyn's not her lawyer. She just said she knew you."

He wasn't sure why that bothered him, but it did.

"Oh yes," Adrianos practically hummed. "We know each other."

Yeah, it definitely bothered him.

"Second," Brunelle forged on, "that's not really the test. There are plenty of gang-banger thugs in the jail who refuse to even talk to their 'public pretender.' The defense attorney has to try the case without any assistance from their client. That doesn't make the defendant incompetent."

"Doesn't it?" Adrianos challenged. "I would suggest that their anger and resentment at both society in general and their government-sponsored lawyer in particular would be symptomatic of a deep-seated personality disorder, likely caused by severe and/or repeated childhood trauma. I imagine most such defendants would present with Oppositional Defiant Disorder or perhaps even Antisocial Personality Disorder, both of which are psychological illnesses recognized in the DSM-IV."

Brunelle just stared at Adrianos, certain he must have misheard him.

"The DSM-IV is the standard diagnostic manual for the fields of psychology and psychiatry," Adrianos explained. "It stands for the Diagnostic and Statistical Manual of Mental Disorders, fourth edition."

Brunelle regained himself. "I know what the DSM-IV is," he assured. "I have a copy on my bookshelf."

Adrianos smiled and nodded. "Of course you do."

"Well, Keesha Sawyer doesn't have Oppositional Defiance Disorder," Brunelle forged on. "She's having no trouble speaking with her attorney, or the doctors at Western State, or me, for that matter."

"Yes, but her delusions of justification," Adrianos said slowly, as if that might help Brunelle understand, "make such conversations unhelpful. Therefore, she cannot assist her attorney. Therefore, she is incompetent."

Brunelle ran his hands through his hair. "But by your definition of incompetency, we'd never reach a verdict of not guilty by reason of insanity. Everyone who's legally insane would also be incompetent and therefore couldn't be prosecuted."

Adrianos smiled. "Exactly.

"But that's crazy."

Adrianos dropped his steepled hands. "Did you really just say that?" he laughed. "Come now. Don't be so upset. It really does make sense if you think about it."

"I don't think it makes sense to render the insanity defense meaningless."

"Of course it does," Adrianos replied evenly. "We render diagnoses irrelevant all the time as the field progresses. Why, did you know that homosexuality used to be a recognized mental disorder? It was in the DSM-II."

Brunelle did know that. Both sides always used that fact to discredit the DSM diagnoses of the other side's psychologist.

"Insanity is outdated," Adrianos declared. "Tell me, what's the seminal legal case on insanity?"

"M'Naghten," Brunelle replied. Everybody knew that. Well, every criminal trial lawyer. "It was a British case from 1840-something. It established the M'Naghten Rule: basically, a defendant can't be found guilty of a crime if he didn't understand the wrongfulness of his conduct."

"Correct," Adrianos affirmed, much to Brunelle's irritation. He didn't need a psychologist to affirm his knowledge of the law. "But it's almost two hundred years old. It's from a bygone era when the English reduced the 'mac' and 'mc' from Scottish and Irish to just an 'M' and an apostrophe. No one does that anymore. And the notion of legal insanity is just as outdated. If someone is so mentally ill that they think it's okay to murder their mother with a hatchet, there is no way they can truly understand the world around them and assist their attorney. Accordingly, they're incompetent. We never reach the question of legal insanity. Such is the progression of the field since 1843."

Brunelle sighed and rested his forehead in a fist. He looked out at the courtyard again. The flower flasher had moved on to a nearby tree and seemed to be doing more than just exposing himself.

"Are you okay, Mr. Brunelle?" Adrianos asked.

Brunelle turned back and smiled weakly. "Sure. It's just— Well, I think you're totally wrong. I was hoping talking to you in person might help, but I guess not. It's just a little disappointing is all."

Adrianos nodded sympathetically. "Yes, I understand. You have a very stressful job."

Brunelle shrugged. "I like my job."

"Of course you do," the doctor replied. "And I hear you're very good at it."

Brunelle smiled. "Yeah? Well, that's nice to hear."

"But that doesn't mean it isn't stressful," Adrianos continued. "Dealing with all those murders and rapes and assaults. Having victims and families depending on you to bring about justice. Only to have people like me get in your way."

Brunelle shook his head. "No, you're just doing your job too."

Adrianos returned his steepled fingertips to his lips. "You know, police officers often seek counseling to help deal with all the horrible things they encounter every day. But I don't see many prosecutors do that."

"I'm not a cop," Brunelle was quick to point out. He helped them, he was part of their team, but he'd never lay claim to that kind of status. Cops were heroes; he was just a lawyer.

"That doesn't mean you couldn't benefit from some counseling yourself."

Brunelle looked out the window again. Apparently the

romantic liaison with the tree was over. The patient was being escorted away by the nurses who had finished their cigarette break.

Brunelle looked back at the psychologist. "I'm not crazy," he insisted.

Adrianos smiled broadly, his eyes flashing disturbingly. "Isn't that exactly what Keesha Sawyer said?"

CHAPTER 13

Adrianos didn't take long to draft his report, but it couldn't have arrived at a worse time. Duncan had scheduled a nine o'clock meeting with Brunelle and Fargas and Fargas' clients. Or rather, Fargas had demanded a meeting with Duncan and Brunelle. Brunelle had received the email scheduler a few days earlier and dutifully accepted it into his busy calendar. So when 8:58 rolled around that morning, Brunelle took a long, last drag of his coffee and trudged into Duncan's office.

"Behave yourself," was all Duncan said when Brunelle walked in.

Brunelle raised his right hand. "So help me God."

Three minutes later, the receptionist escorted Fargas and his clients into Duncan's office. The introductions commenced and soon Brunelle learned that the couple's names were Louise and Ron Langford. They all sat down around the conference table and Duncan started the meeting.

"So, what can we do for you, Charles?"

Fargas leaned back and grinned. He was far more

comfortable being catered to than being challenged. Brunelle just sat quietly, arms crossed, and told himself, *Shut up, Brunelle. Just shut up.*

"I've got some concerns, Matt," Fargas started. He gestured toward Mr. and Mrs. Langford. "*We* have some concerns. About the way the criminal case is proceeding."

Duncan nodded and turned to Brunelle. "How is it proceeding?"

"It isn't," Brunelle replied. "We're in a holding pattern until the competency issue gets sorted out."

Duncan would understand that. Fargas, apparently, not so much.

"That's where our concerns lie, Matt," he said. "This is off to a slow start and going nowhere fast. I wonder—*We* wonder, whether the case might need to be reassigned to someone who will be a little more aggressive."

Brunelle's fists clenched. He didn't get taken off cases. He got put on cases when other attorneys got taken off them. And he certainly didn't get taken off cases because he didn't suck up to some fat-ass civil attorney. The voice in his head that had told him to shut up, threw up its hands and said, *Yeah, never mind. Say whatever you want.*

Luckily, Duncan jumped in first. "I appreciate your concerns, Charles, but these things take time. Mental health defenses are especially complicated and slow. We need to wait for the competency evaluation, then we can move forward."

"Well, that's just it," Fargas blustered. "We have the competency evaluation. The doctors said she's competent, so I don't understand—" He waved again at Mr. and Mrs. Langford. "*We* don't understand why Keesha hasn't been arraigned yet. At this rate, the case will never go to trial."

Duncan looked to Brunelle. "Dave?"

"The defense is getting an independent eval." Brunelle knew Duncan didn't need any more explanation for the delay than that.

"Really?" Duncan remarked. It wasn't that common. Usually, they accepted the Western State evaluation.

"Really," Brunelle confirmed. "They have that right. It's in the statute."

Duncan nodded and turned to Fargas. "He's right."

Fargas narrowed his eyes and started to blotch red at the jowls. The guy obviously had a temper. Brunelle guessed he lost it a lot in trial. If he ever went to trial.

"Well, how long is *that* going to take?" Fargas demanded.

A knock came on Duncan's door. All eyes turned to see Nicole opening the door, several sheets of paper in her hand. "This just came in by email," she said to Brunelle. "I thought you'd want to see it."

Duncan seemed a bit irritated by the interruption, but Brunelle knew what it was—the only thing Nicole would have interrupted that particular meeting for. He stood up and took the report from her. "Thanks."

She smiled and offered a subtle wink. "Good luck," she whispered.

Brunelle closed the door as he scanned the top sheet. He nodded and looked at the others. "Yep. This is their report."

"What does it say?" Duncan asked.

Brunelle flipped through it quickly. He knew what it was going to say, but he also knew he better confirm it before he said it out loud. Luckily, Adrianos wrote a much clearer report than the folks at Western State. Three pages, right to the point, with the conclusion in boldface at the end. "They say she's incompetent."

Fargas threw his arms wide and made a loud noise like a tire going flat. "Well, now what?!"

"Now we have a contested competency hearing," Brunelle answered. "With dueling experts. Our doc says she's competent. Theirs says she isn't. And the judge decides.

"What if the judge agrees with their expert, Mr. Brunelle?" Mrs. Langford asked. "What if the judge decides she's incompetent."

Brunelle frowned. "Then the case will be dismissed."

CHAPTER 14

Kat was in a side room off the examining area. She was sitting at a small table on which rested an open jar of cloudy green liquid, a human brain on a metal tray, and her sack lunch.

She looked up as Brunelle darkened the doorway, a scalpel in one hand, the last bite of a B.L.T. in the other.

"David!" She stuffed the food in her mouth and swallowed. "To what do I owe this unexpected pleasure?"

"You're eating lunch?" Brunelle was a bit shocked.

Kat shrugged. "Busy day. I'm working through lunch."

Brunelle shook his head. "I didn't mean working through lunch. I meant, how the hell can you eat with a dead brain on a plate in front of you?"

Kat looked down at the half-dissected organ. "It's a tray," she pointed out.

Brunelle laughed. "Oh, right. Of course. Forgive my ignorance."

Kat slid the brain away and set down her scalpel. "Okay, Mr. Squeamish, would you like to leave this room to discuss whatever it is you've come by to discuss?"

Brunelle didn't like the squeamish comment. "No, that's fine. I probably should have called first anyway. I was just thinking about the Sawyer case. Sometimes I can't stop thinking like a lawyer, so I thought I'd come by and pick a non-lawyer's brain."

Kat picked up the scalpel again and pointed at the wrinkled, gray lump on her table. "He was a bus driver. Be my guest."

Brunelle groaned. "Is that medical examiner humor?"

"You gotta have a sense of humor to do this job."

Brunelle shrugged. He supposed that was true.

"I'd think you'd need one for your job too," Kat said. "But you seem like you've lost yours today."

Brunelle waved it away. "Naw." He made sure to smile. "I'm just contemplating what kind of woman my girlfriend is."

Kat smiled. "Girlfriend," she repeated. "I do like it when you call me that. I guess that makes you my boyfriend."

Brunelle laughed. "Boyfriend, huh? Not too many boys have gray in their hair."

Kat shrugged. "Well, how many girls do you know with teenage daughters?"

Brunelle considered the cases he'd seen over his career, defendants and victims alike. *More than there ought to be,* he thought.

"Never mind." Kat must have seen the expression on his face. "I don't want to know. What can I do for you today, Mr. Mopey?"

Brunelle felt stung. He wasn't mopey. Just preoccupied, serious. And no one likes to be called names. But he decided to ignore it.

"I'm just having trouble wrapping my head around the defense argument," he explained. "And if I can't do that, I can't rebut it properly. I met with their doc and he says she's incompetent because she's so sure what she did was justified that she can't assist her attorney."

Kat protruded a thoughtful lip. "I guess that makes sense."

Brunelle shook his head. "No, it doesn't. See, thinking something unjustified is justified makes you insane, not incompetent. But not guilty by reason of insanity is a verdict at the end of a trial. You never get there if the case is dismissed at the beginning because the defendant is incompetent."

"Okay." Kat shrugged.

Brunelle frowned. "I'm wondering if maybe I should call you at the competency hearing. You could explain just how intentional the killing was."

Kat raised her palms. "Whoa, big fella. I've never testified at a competency hearing before. That's for head-shrinkers, not head-carvers."

Brunelle crossed his arms and tapped his lips. She had a point. He was grasping at straws. Adrianos had him flustered. *Damn it.*

"So is that the only reason you came by?" Kat asked. "It seems like you could have asked me that over the phone."

"Oh." Brunelle shook himself out of his thoughts about the case. "Yeah, right. Well, I guess I wanted to see you too."

"I guess, he says." Kat laughed. "What a boyfriend. Well, I guess I like seeing you too."

Brunelle smiled. But he felt like he was being teased. He didn't like it.

"And another thing," Kat pressed good-naturedly. "You're always talking about your work. We never talk about us anymore."

"Us?" Brunelle repeated. "I think I'm still getting used to there being an 'us.'"

Kat smiled—that deep luscious smile that made her eyes

smolder. "Get used to it, boyfriend."

Brunelle liked that look. "So what should we talk about us?"

Kat's smile twisted at one corner. "How about us at a museum?"

"Museum?" Brunelle wasn't thinking about anything even close to a museum. "What museum?"

"S.A.M. The Seattle Art Museum. They're having a Rauschenburg exhibit."

"Sounds contagious," Brunelle quipped.

"Tsk, tsk, David," Kat admonished. "Don't sound so pedestrian. You can be it, just don't sound it. He's Lizzy's favorite painter. We're going next Saturday. I want you to come."

It wasn't a request. Brunelle knew it.

"Okay," he said. "Us. Lizzy. Museum. Rauschenburg virus."

"Exhibit," Kat laughed. "You jackass."

"Exhibit," he confirmed. "You know, you're not the first woman to call me a jackass."

Kat raised an eyebrow. "You really want to go there?"

Brunelle thought for a moment. "No. No, I don't. So, what time on Saturday?"

"The museum opens at ten."

"Ugh, that's early. Okay. Should I just meet you there?"

"No." Kat grinned.

"No?"

"No," Kat purred. "We'll all leave together after you roll out of my bed and make breakfast for us."

Brunelle smiled. He liked the sound of that. "Us."

Kat locked her eyes on his. "Us."

CHAPTER 15

The contested competency hearing was scheduled three weeks out. The lawyers needed time to prepare and the doctors had very busy schedules. Professional courtesy prevented Brunelle and Edwards from simply picking a date and issuing. Instead, the date was selected when everyone was available and the hearing was scheduled for nine a.m. in front of Judge Harold Perry.

It was Perry's last term. He'd been a judge since before Brunelle got his bar card. He'd presided over some of the county's most high-profile trials. And he probably should have retired about five years earlier. But, on the promise he wouldn't run again, he ran unopposed one last time—no one ever filed against the great and powerful Judge Perry—and was allowed to ride off into the sunset of a memorable and accomplished judicial career. But first, he would preside over Keesha Sawyer's competency hearing.

Brunelle arrived about fifteen minutes early for the hearing. Time enough to set up his things on his counsel table and pour a cup of water to lubricate the questions and arguments he'd be making over the better part of the day.

It also gave him time to check in with his expert, Gregory Thompson, Ph.D. He was youngish, with strawberry blond hair and a struggling beard. Brunelle was beginning to notice that more and more people he encountered professionally were younger than him. Thompson was sitting on a bench in the hallway, reviewing his report.

"Dr. Thompson," Brunelle greeted the psychologist and extended a hand. "Thanks for coming in this morning."

Thompson stood and shook Brunelle's hand. "Of course. Thank you for accommodating my schedule." He looked at his watch. "How long will this take?"

"The entire hearing will probably take all day," Brunelle answered. "But you should only be on the stand for an hour or so."

"Only," Thompson scoffed. "That seems like an awfully long time to explain one simple issue."

Brunelle smiled. "Nothing's simple when you get lawyers involved. The defense will put on their own expert after you who'll say she's incompetent. Then we'll spend all afternoon arguing about who's right and why, only to have the judge announce a decision he probably already made before he even took the bench."

Thompson shook his head. "What a strange system. Having a judge with no medical or psychological training decide a mental health issue makes no sense."

"Maybe not," Brunelle agreed. "But that's what you guys are for. You're witnesses. You give the judge your opinions, then he decides. You can't both be right, so someone has to decide who to believe, you or Adrianos."

"Adrianos?" Thompson's eyes widened. "Peter Adrianos? That's the other psychologist?"

"Yes," Brunelle answered cautiously. "Do you know him?"

"I know *of* him," Thompson answered with a chuckle. "He's nuts."

Brunelle raised an eyebrow. "Really?" Adrianos had certainly seemed full of himself, but not actually crazy or anything.

"Well, not clinically," Thompson clarified. "But he's a little out there with his thinking. He used to do some other stuff before he got into psychology, so that informs his thinking sometimes."

"Oh yeah?" Brunelle replied. "What other stuff?"

Thompson laughed. "I think he used to be a lawyer."

* * *

"All rise!"

Judge Perry's bailiff pounded the gavel as the aged jurist took the bench. None of the other judges actually pounded a gavel anymore, but Perry had become a judge back when they still did and he'd be damned if he was going to stop now.

Perry sat down with some effort—back pain, well known by the attorneys thanks to the whispers that fill a courthouse's hallways. He had a shock of thick white hair and a full white beard. It was generally accepted that Judge Adams had grown his beard in an attempt to look like a young Perry.

The judge fumbled a bit with the pleadings his bailiff had left on the bench for him, then he looked up. "Are the parties ready on the matter of the State of Washington versus, uh," he looked down at the name again, "Keesha Sawyer?"

"Yes, Your Honor," Brunelle answered, being sure to stand to address the court.

"The defense is ready," Edwards announced. The corrections officers—they didn't like being called 'guards'—had brought Keesha in the secure side hallway about two minutes before Perry took the bench. Edwards had managed a very brief, whispering consultation with her client. That is, Edwards had whispered. Keesha hadn't seen the need apparently. She'd answered rather loudly in fact, and Brunelle had had no difficulty hearing her protestations.

"But I am competent."

"It was self defense."

"I want to go to trial."

Brunelle smiled and wished the rules allowed the State to call a defendant to the stand. He knew Edwards would never let her testify. He'd have to hope for some sort of helpful outburst.

The courtroom was mostly empty. The only people in the gallery were Dr. Thompson, waiting to testify, a lone reporter from the local paper, and, much to Brunelle's surprise and delight, Robyn Dunn.

She smiled and waved when Brunelle noticed her. "Hiya, Mr. B.," she said with a wink.

Brunelle smiled and nodded back. He wasn't much of a winker.

Adrianos, Edwards had informed him, would be arriving around ten. Usually, dueling experts listened to each other's testimony, so they could call bullshit on each other. Apparently, Adrianos didn't feel the need to do that. He really was an arrogant S.O.B.

"Would the court like a brief opening statement before we begin with the witnesses?" Brunelle asked.

Perry scowled. "I don't need you two to tell me what the issues are or how I should rule. I know what the issues are and I know how you want me to rule. I've done more of these competency hearings than you two combined. You put on your witnesses, counsel, and I'll make my decision."

Brunelle offered a contrite, "Yes, Your Honor," then looked to Edwards.

"Here we go," he whispered.

Edwards nodded. "Yep, here we go."

Brunelle looked up at Perry, still glowering down at them. "The State calls Dr. Gregory Thompson."

CHAPTER 16

Brunelle didn't waste a lot of time on the introductory stuff. If there'd been a jury, he would have had Thompson lay out all his credentials and degrees and certificates and everything else to establish his bona fides. As it was, Brunelle simply had him identify himself as a staff psychologist at Western State Hospital. That would be enough for Perry.

Then straight to business. He'd examined Keesha Sawyer. He'd asked her all the right questions and she'd given all the right answers. She knew what she'd done, what she was charged with, and what she was facing. She knew Brunelle was the prosecutor, Edwards was her lawyer, and the old guy on the bench was the judge. She might be insane, but she was competent.

"Thank you, doctor," Brunelle said as he finished up. "No further questions."

Edwards stood up and stepped casually toward the witness stand. "Good morning, doctor."

"Good morning," Thompson replied.

Edwards was clearly relaxed. There was no jury—a judge

made the competency determination alone—so the lawyers could relax a bit and enjoy matching wits with a witness without the added pressure of acting a role for the jury. "So, you believe my client is competent to stand trial?"

Thompson thought for a split-second before answering. Brunelle liked that. "Yes."

"And that's based on your assessment that she understands the charges against her and the nature of the prosecution?"

Again, Thompson thought for a moment before answering. "Yes."

"But there's another part of the equation, isn't there, doctor? She also has to have the ability to assist her attorney, isn't that true?"

Thompson nodded, lower lip protruding thoughtfully. "That is true. And I observed nothing that would suggest she lacked the ability to do so."

Edwards nodded. She pointed her pen absently at the psychologist. "She believes she was justified in killing her mother, doesn't she?"

Before Thompson could answer, Keesha offered a loud. "Uh-huh. That's right." Edwards spun around and hushed her, a finger raised to her lips. Keesha nodded, a bit wide-eyed, and acknowledged her lawyer's instructions with a pantomime zipper across her lips.

Edwards returned her attention to the witness.

"Could you repeat the question?" he asked.

"My client has a fixed belief that the killing of her mother was justified, isn't that right?"

Thompson did his split-second thinking bit, then answered, "Yes, that's right. That particular idea is quite fixed in her thinking."

Edwards threw her arms wide. "Then how can she possibly assist in her own defense?"

Thompson cocked his head. "I don't understand the question."

Edward crossed her arms. "How can my client possibly assist me in defending her if she has a fixed delusion that the killing was justified because her mother was turning her into a zombie?"

"And the neighborhood children too, I believe," Thompson added.

"Yes, thank you," Edwards replied. "And the neighborhood children too. You don't expect me to try to get the jury to believe that was actually going on, do you?"

Thompson shook his head. "No, ma'am. I don't imagine that would be very effective."

"Exactly." Another, more forceful jab with her pen to accentuate her point. "So how can she assist me?"

Thompson thought for several seconds. Finally, he said, "Well, as I understand it, you're a very experienced criminal defense attorney. You're the one trained in the law and who knows all the defenses and who can explain it all to the jury. I'm sure you've had more than one client who lied to you or was otherwise unhelpful, but that didn't make them incompetent."

Bravo, thought Brunelle.

Edwards frowned. "Let me try it a different way." She gestured toward the witness stand. "Can you help me by handing me that banana there?"

Thompson looked around where he was sitting. There were definitely no bananas anywhere near him. "Excuse me?"

"That banana right there," Edwards repeated, still pointing, but looking away as if bored. "Right there in front of you."

Thompson regarded his area again. "You mean the microphone?" he asked, laying a hand on the stand of the device in front of him.

"That's not a microphone, my good doctor," Edwards replied, turning back to him. "It's a banana. Could you please hand me the banana?"

Brunelle shook his head. She was being cute. Perry hated cute. He supposed he could have objected, but decided to let Edwards take enough rope to hang herself.

Thompson sighed. "I see what you're trying to do, but regardless, it's a microphone."

"How can you help me with the banana," Edwards asked, "if you can't even see that it's a banana?"

"Because it's not a banana," Thompson replied. "It's a microphone."

"I say it's a banana," Edwards said. "Ms. Sawyer says it was justified."

"You're both wrong," Thompson replied. "And I'm the sane one, so I can explain to the judge that this is a microphone and not a banana. When the time comes to discuss the murder at the trial, I imagine you'll do the same for the jury."

Edwards huffed. Her trick wasn't working. "Look, just hand me the banana and we can move on to my other questions."

Before Thompson could reply, Perry leaned down from the bench. "You have no more questions, Ms. Edwards."

"But I do, Your Honor," she protested, not comprehending the judge's proclamation.

"No," he said. "You don't. Sit down."

Edwards hesitated, but only for a moment. "Yes, Your Honor." She'd made her point, such as it was.

"Any re-direct examination, Mr. Brunelle?" Perry invited.

"Just briefly, Your Honor." Brunelle stood up and gestured to the microphone. "Doctor, could you hand me that orange?"

Thompson's face twisted into a puzzled expression.

"Orange?"

Brunelle grinned. "Orange you glad I didn't say banana?"

The corrections officer laughed. The judge didn't. "Sit down, Mr. Brunelle."

He did as he was told.

Edwards looked over at him and shook her head. "You're such a jackass," she whispered.

Brunelle smiled. "So I hear."

"Who's the next witness?" Perry demanded as Dr. Thompson stepped down form the witness stand.

"I am!" boomed a voice from the doorway. All eyes turned to the tall, handsome man who'd just thrown the doors open. "Dr. Peter Adrianos, Your Honor. Ready to educate the court."

Brunelle grinned to himself. *Oh, this ought to be good.*

CHAPTER 17

After Edwards rushed over to Adrianos and whispered frantically in his ear—likely to shut the hell up—she pointed to the witness stand and announced, "The defense calls Dr. Peter Adrianos."

The psychologist sauntered to the stand, offering Brunelle a nod and Robyn a wink as he approached the judge and raised his right hand.

Perry's right hand was also raised. "Do you solemnly swear or affirm that the testimony you will give in this proceeding is the truth, the whole truth, and nothing but the truth?"

"Without question," Adrianos replied.

Brunelle shook his head. *How about a simple 'yes'?*

He looked up at Edwards, preparing to start her exam. "Now who's the jackass?" he whispered.

"Oh, you're still the jackass," she whispered back without looking at him. "He's my expert."

Brunelle smiled and picked up his pen to take notes of Adrianos' direct.

Edwards didn't skimp on the credentials. Adrianos wasn't from the state hospital, so she knew Perry would start off discounting his opinion. His education seemed impressive enough, although not as impressive as to justify his overly confident demeanor. B.A. from a state university. Master's from a different one. Ph.D. from a small private school in Ohio. No law degree, Brunelle noted with some relief. Maybe Adrianos wasn't such a narcissist after all.

Then the usual litany of jobs and positions, including an internship at Western State Hospital. Then off to Cascade Mental Hospital where he'd worked his way up from staff psychologist to manager to assistant director and finally director. He had a vision for the place, he said.

Great.

Perry didn't seem particularly impressed. In fact, he seemed bored, even drowsy. Brunelle had heard the stories about how Perry had been a real spitfire when he'd first taken the bench. But decades of being overturned on appeal and old-fashioned aging had left a tired shell of a man. Brunelle thought he might actually be nodding off.

Edwards was too involved in her questioning to notice. "Now, doctor, did you have an opportunity to conduct a mental health examination of my client, Keesha Sawyer?"

Adrianos folded his hands importantly in front of him. "Yes. Yes, I did."

"And what was your conclusion regarding my client's competency to stand trial?"

Adrianos nodded and looked up to the judge to deliver his earth-shattering conclusion. But Perry had his chin on his hand and his eyes closed.

"Ah," Adrianos stammered. He looked back to Edwards. "I

concluded that Ms. Sawyer is incompetent to stand trial."

"And what is that conclusion based on, doctor?"

Adrianos looked up at Perry again. He appeared visibly irritated that the judge wasn't riveted by his testimony. "I'm sorry," he turned back to Edwards. "What was your question?"

Edwards finally became aware of Perry's dozing. She looked up to where Adrianos had been staring and sighed. Glancing around for something suitable, she fetched her three-ring binder from her counsel table and promptly dropped it to the floor.

Thud!

Without looking up at the suddenly awake Judge Perry, Edwards bent down and picked up her binder. "Oh, I'm sorry, Your Honor. How clumsy of me."

She set the binder back on her table and returned her attention to Adrianos. She never looked at the judge who was wiping his lips and checking for drool.

"So anyway, doctor," Edwards continued. "You said you found my client incompetent to stand trial. Could you explain the basis for your conclusion?"

Brunelle was impressed. Not only had she awakened the judge without embarrassing him, but the old man now stared down at Adrianos, awaiting the psychologist's response with exaggerated interest, to compensate for his previously unconscious state.

Adrianos was aware of this extra focus and took advantage of it. He launched into the same explanation he'd given Brunelle at Cascade. It was impossible, absolutely impossible, for Keesha to assist her lawyer because she was convinced, wrongly, that her actions were justified, thereby precluding the presentation of a potentially more effective defense.

"Thank you, doctor," Edwards concluded. "No further questions."

Perry nodded, exaggerating his frown of thoughtfulness. He looked to Brunelle. "Any cross examination?"

"Yes, Your Honor." Brunelle stood up and buttoned his suit coat. "Thank you."

He walked up to the witness stand. "Good to see you again, doctor," he started. It wasn't really, but he wanted the judge to know he'd done his homework.

Adrianos nodded. "You too, counselor." Brunelle knew he was lying too. *Good.* They understood each other.

"Now, you've just testified that Ms. Sawyer's belief that she was justified in killing her mother is the cause of her incompetency to stand trial, correct?"

Adrianos shifted in his seat. "That's a bit oversimplified and not very artfully stated, but basically correct."

Brunelle smirked at the description of his question. He decided to ignore that part of it. Instead he continued on toward the point of his cross exam. "And you're familiar with the definition of legal insanity, correct?"

"Yes," Adrianos returned Brunelle's smile. He obviously knew where Brunelle was going. They both did. They'd already had the conversation, only Perry hadn't been there, so they had to do it again. "A person is legally insane if he or she doesn't appreciate the wrongfulness of their conduct."

"Correct," Brunelle confirmed. "So shouldn't that question be put to the jury at the end of the trial, as we've done for over a century, rather than short-circuiting the process at the beginning by declaring the person incompetent to stand trial, thereby precluding any prosecution at all?"

Adrianos nodded patiently, like a parent with a slow child. His challenging grin melted into a serious expression. "That's a very fair question, Mr. Brunelle." He looked up at Judge Perry, who—to

Brunelle's disappointment—was still staring at Edwards' witness with far too much interest. Adrianos did have a way about him. A definite charm. "Psychology is a dynamic, ever-changing field. We learn more every day about the human mind. The M'Naghten standard is well over one hundred years old. When it was adopted, slavery was legal and women couldn't vote. We've moved away from those deplorable social standards and we must be willing to move away from equally outdated psychological standards."

Brunelle frowned. He was losing control of the examination. "But you agree that the M'Naghten rule is the standard. You're just advocating that this judge ignore it and establish a new standard. The Adrianos Standard."

Adrianos turned back to Brunelle and smiled broadly. He clearly liked the idea of a new legal standard being named after him.

"Let me answer your question this way," the psychologist said. "There is a long held prejudice that people can be classified into two categories, mentally ill and not mentally ill. Us and them. Right and wrong. But in truth, everyone has psychological issues they deal with. Whether it's resentment for growing up with a workaholic father or auditory and visual hallucinations from severe schizophrenia. Metal illness is a continuum, not distinct categories of sane and insane.

"I dare say," he went on, "that everyone in this room has diagnosable emotional and personality pathologies." He pointed at Brunelle. "Take you, for example. You came to my hospital and pretended to not understand something you clearly understand very well. You were trying to deceive me to get a particular result you wanted. That is highly manipulative, and you probably don't even realize you're doing it. Now, here you are, seeking justice and playing hero, reveling in the recognition and affirmation while caring little to nothing about the underlying crime itself. A classic case of Narcissistic Personality Disorder."

Brunelle was taken aback by the instant diagnosis thrown at him.

Adrianos grinned at him. "You probably have a 'Prosecutor of the Year' plaque on your office wall, don't you?"

Brunelle had to smile back. "I have two."

Adrianos surrendered a small laugh, then pointed at Edwards. "And then we have Ms. Edwards. A 'true believer,' I think you called her. Not in it for the money clearly if she's a public defender, and dedicated enough to have distinguished herself and earned the right to represent murder defendants. But she doesn't get the cocktail party affirmation you do, Mr. Brunelle. You get to bathe in the admiration and thank-yous you receive for your profession, but Ms. Edwards has to weather the subtle scorn and derision she encounters for representing criminals. 'How can you do that?' is probably the most common question she gets after telling someone what she does. But the real question is *why* does she do it? The answer is that she's trying to save everyone in the world, one murderer at a time. Maybe she suffered some childhood trauma where she watched a friend drown in a pool, or couldn't pull her mother out of a debilitating depression brought about by an abusive, alcoholic father. Maybe, her subconscious tells her with every case, maybe if she gets Keesha acquitted, maybe this time mom will come out of her darkened bedroom today."

Edwards jaw dropped at the description. Brunelle didn't want to know if any of that was even close to true. Adrianos didn't give him the chance to ask. He turned and looked up at Perry.

"Even the judge clearly has problems. Obviously, anyone who wants to be a judge has huge control issues. Even as you sit and doze atop your ridiculously elevated bench, you are in charge.

You can sit back and do nothing, yet everything that happens in your courtroom does so because you allow it. Indeed, the word 'court' comes from the tradition that the king, the sovereign of all he surveyed, resolved all the differences in his kingdom, his subjects coming to his court to plead their cases. Judges have had this absolute power delegated to them, and we all have to stand up when you walk in and call you 'Your Honor.'"

Adrianos turned back to Brunelle. "So, yes. I would say it's time to abandon the prejudices of the past, and with them the legal standards that branded someone 'insane' when, in reality, that term has no meaning in modern psychology. We are all mentally ill to one degree or another. We need to focus on healing the most affected rather than punishing them."

Brunelle nodded, not because he agreed, but because he was satisfied he didn't need to ask any more questions. Adrianos had called Perry a control freak. He had no idea. Perry was about to prove it.

"No further questions."

Perry didn't even ask Edwards if she had any re-direct examination.

"You may step down," he told Adrianos. Then he looked to Edwards. Brunelle knew it was good that he was looking at her. Perry always delivered his ruling directly to the losing lawyer. "I find the defendant competent." That was it. No explanation, just the ruling. "The matter will proceed to trial."

Edwards started to protest, but Perry cut her off, now directing his comments to both lawyers. "In addition," he declared, "this matter will be assigned to my courtroom for trial. We will hold a status conference in one week for the parties to update me on their readiness for trial. Be prepared to list all witnesses and endorse whatever defenses you may choose. Dr. Adrianos may think insanity is outdated and that this humble trial court should trump the legislature and the appellate courts, but I disagree. If you plan to pursue an insanity defense, be prepared to announce it at the status conference." Then he stood and banged his gavel. "Court is adjourned."

The judge marched down the steps of his ridiculously elevated bench and stormed back into his chambers.

Brunelle stepped over to Edwards. "That went well."

"Oh, shut up, Dave," Edwards replied. She was in no mood for his jokes. Brunelle wondered what bothered her the most: having lost the hearing, having just drawn Perry as the trial judge, or Adrianos' drive-by diagnosis of her.

Brunelle decided to heed Edwards' advice and returned to gathering up his own things from his counsel table. For his part, he was pleased to have gotten Perry as his trial judge. He was the last of a dying breed: hard-ass, pro-prosecution judges. Brunelle could expect to win most of his motions and objections now.

As he was picking up his things, Adrianos walked past his table. "I don't believe the judge was impressed by my testimony," he remarked.

"On the contrary," Brunelle replied, "your testimony made quite the impression. You totally pissed him off."

Adrianos narrowed his eyes and looked up now at the empty judge's bench. "Did you manipulate me into that as well?"

Brunelle shook his head. "I'm not that good, doctor. I just ask questions and people answer. Generally, people say what they want to say. I just give them the chance to do it."

CHAPTER 18

Brunelle watched Adrianos leave, then scanned the gallery for Robyn. But she'd already left too. He was more disappointed than he knew he should be. Edwards was still at work, sitting at her table trying to explain the judge's ruling to her client. From what he could hear, it was more like Edwards was trying to explain why the ruling was bad for them. But Keesha seemed happy. She wanted to go to trial. The jury would understand. She couldn't let the kids be turned into zombies.

Brunelle shook his head as he left the courtroom. Maybe Edwards would pursue that insanity defense after all. When he got upstairs to his office, the first person he told about winning the hearing was Nicole.

"Good for you, David," she beamed. "I knew you had it in you."

Brunelle paused at the turn of phrase. Before he could think of something not inappropriate to reply, Nicole inclined her head toward Duncan's office. "You better tell the boss. Mr. Fargas has been blowing up his phone all morning."

Brunelle frowned at the mention of the civil attorney's name. He'd been riding a high from his victory, but the thought of that walrus with a bar card brought him crashing down. "Right," he forced himself to say. "Will do."

He passed his own office and went straight to Duncan's. Duncan was on the phone, so Brunelle knocked on the doorframe and gave a thumbs-up when Duncan looked his way.

"Actually, Charles," Duncan said into the phone, "he just stepped into my office. I'll get the details and call you right back. Yes. Right. I will. Okay. Bye."

He hung up the phone and sighed. "That guy is really something."

"Yeah, something," Brunelle agreed enigmatically. "Anyway, we won the competency hearing."

"Fargas will be glad to hear that."

"And we got Perry for the trial," Brunelle was pleased to inform his boss.

Duncan's expression moved from simple relief to actual pleasure. "Really? That's a great draw."

Brunelle laughed. "Yeah, the defense psychologist pissed him off so much he decided to keep the case for trial too."

Duncan smiled. "What did the guy say that pissed him off so much?"

"He told Perry he was a control freak."

"He is a control freak," Duncan laughed.

"He also called him out for falling asleep on the bench."

"Ouch," Duncan said. "No wonder he kept the case. He can manage it to make sure the defendant gets convicted."

"That's kind of what I'm hoping for," Brunelle admitted. "Although..."

"Although what?" Duncan narrowed suspicious eyes.

"Perry set a status conference next week and all but ordered Jessica to endorse an insanity defense," Brunelle explained. "If she does that, it'll be hard to beat."

"No, no," Duncan waved the idea away. "You can't let that happen. We do not want an NGRI."

"Why not?" Brunelle asked with a shrug. "Seems like that might be the most just result."

"We've been through this, Dave. Your job is to get a conviction."

"We've been through this, Matt," Brunelle agreed. "My job is justice."

"I know that," Duncan bristled. "But until and unless they endorse insanity, the only just result is guilty."

Brunelle nodded. "I suppose that's true. And don't worry too much. Jessica's as stubborn as Perry. Now that he's told her to endorse it, there's no way she will."

"Good," Duncan replied. Then he looked at his phone. "I suppose I better call Fargas."

Brunelle shrugged. "Guess so. At least you have good news for him. May I be excused for that call?"

Duncan nodded. "Sure. He doesn't like you anyway."

Brunelle laughed as he stood up. "Good."

* * *

A short time later, Brunelle was at his desk, dialing Chen's number to tell him about winning the hearing.

"Chen."

"Larry, it's Brunelle. We won the competency hearing."

"Hey, good job," Chen said. "I knew you weren't that bad an attorney."

"Very funny, Detective," Brunelle replied. "I'll have you know—"

Beep-beep! Brunelle's phone went off. He had a new text.

"Hold on," he said, pulling out his phone. "Aw geez. Kat just texted me."

"Why 'aw geez'? I thought she was your girlfriend."

"Ugh," Brunelle said. "I'm still not totally comfortable with that word."

"How's 'ladyfriend'?" Chen suggested.

Brunelle laughed. "Even worse."

"So why the 'aw geez'?" Chen persisted.

Brunelle hesitated. "I dunno. It's just, we have plans tonight. Nothing big. Just dinner. She just texted me to say she'll be late."

"Oh," Chen said. "So you're disappointed you won't see her sooner?"

"No, I'm disappointed I'm going out at all. I was going to work late. I need to draft up the written order for Perry to sign, to reduce his oral ruling to writing."

"That'll wait a day, won't it?" Chen asked.

Brunelle shrugged even though Chen wasn't there to see. "I guess so. I just wasn't thinking about her is all."

"Well, maybe you should," Chen advised. "She's worth thinking about."

Brunelle shrugged again. "Yeah. You're right. Of course you're right. Just hard to switch gears so fast sometimes."

"Well, you're old," Chen teased.

"That doesn't help."

"I wasn't trying to help."

"Goodbye, Larry."

"Goodbye, old man. Say hi to your ladyfriend for me."

Brunelle gladly hung up his desk phone and stared at his cell.

bodies stacking up. literally. will be done by 5:30. want me to stop by your office to get u?

He typed his reply: *sure. sounds good. see u then.*

He hit send, then leaned back in his chair. He smiled, but not about Kat. He'd won the hearing.

He looked up at the framed certificates on his wall.

Prosecutor of the Fucking Year.

CHAPTER 19

Shortly before five o'clock, Brunelle's desk phone rang. His caller ID showed it was the front desk receptionist.

"There's a young woman here to see you," the receptionist told him.

Brunelle smiled. Kat must have finished her autopsies early. She wasn't young exactly, but she was younger than him. The receptionist was giving him a good-natured tease about his new ladyfriend.

But when he reached the lobby, he was surprised—and pleased—to see that there really was a young woman there to see him. Robyn Dunn. Looking as heart-racing as ever.

"Robyn," Brunelle managed to say through the pounding in his chest. "This is a surprise."

"I know," she said, fixing her blue eyes on his. "And I know it's five o'clock. Do you have just a minute?"

"Of course," Brunelle answered. "Come on back to my office. I'm working late tonight anyway."

"Of course you are," Robyn said as she slid past him into the back hallways. It made more sense for Brunelle to lead the way to his office, rather than having to give her directions—'turn left,' 'last office on the right'—but they both knew this was a better way for Brunelle to stare at her very nice ass. She usually wore pantsuits, Brunelle had noticed. Seeing how they hugged her curves, he understood why. They reached his office too soon.

Robyn dropped her tall frame into one of Brunelle's visitor chairs. Brunelle sat at his desk. "So what brings you by?" he asked.

Not that I'm complaining, he thought.

She shrugged. "I guess I just wanted to apologize for Peter. He can be kind of an ass sometimes."

Brunelle grinned. "Yeah, he didn't make any friends today, did he? But that's not your fault. No need for you to apologize."

Robyn frowned slightly. "Yeah, well, I feel kind of responsible. It was my idea to bring him on board. And he and I, well, we have history."

Brunelle nodded. He didn't want to hear about their history.

"Well, no worries," he said. "Like you said, he made an ass of himself, and I won the hearing. All in all, a good day for me."

She smiled, that dimple peeking out again. "Actually, I kind of enjoyed watching you make a fool of him. That's why I ran out of court so fast. To see if he was still fuming. I loved it."

She shook her head. "I always took him on head-on, but you just let him talk—God, he likes to talk—and he hanged himself. It was masterful."

Brunelle demurred. "Well, I've been told I can be pretty manipulative."

Robyn lowered her eyelids. "Manipulate just means grabbing things you want and making them move the way you want them to." She locked her eyes on Brunelle's. "No crime in that."

Brunelle didn't say anything for a moment. Not because he

couldn't think of anything to say, but because he knew not to say what he was thinking. He glanced at the clock and realized the time.

Shit.

Kat was never as late as she said she'd be. He didn't want to get caught in his office after hours with a cute young lawyer. He wasn't doing anything, but he was imagining things. And if he could imagine them, so could Kat.

"Well, thanks for stopping by, Robyn," he said suddenly. He stood up, just to make sure she understood the point. "I'm glad you enjoyed the show today."

Robyn looked a little surprised at the abrupt ending to their conversation. Brunelle guessed not many men hurried her departure. "Oh, um, well, yeah. It was fun. Uh, good job." She thought for a moment. "Don't tell Jess I said that."

Brunelle winked; he immediately wished he hadn't. "Our little secret," he said.

Robyn smiled at that. "I think I could handle having some secrets with you."

Brunelle sighed silently to himself. If it weren't for the fact that Robyn was a public defender and the huge complications that would accompany any liaison between them—oh, and the whole Kat thing—he'd be tempted to take her up on her obvious flirting right there in his office. It was after hours, and his door had a lock.

"Spoken like a true attorney," he deflected the meaning behind her comment, then gestured toward the door. He escorted her back to the lobby, once again taking in the scenery of her perfectly wrapped ass, before bidding her goodbye.

* * *

Kat was indeed early. That is, she wasn't as late as she said she'd be. Brunelle got a text at 5:21: *I'm in your lobby. come and get it.*

He smiled. She had a way about her too.

He came out to the lobby and let her in. "Hey, beautiful," he said as she stepped into him for a kiss. He kissed her a little harder and a little longer than she might have expected. She didn't seem to mind.

"Mmm, David," she purred. "Maybe I should have gotten here earlier."

Brunelle kept his poker face. "No, your timing is perfect. Come on back. I'll shut down my computer and grab my coat."

He followed Kat back to his office and remarked to himself that she had a pretty nice ass too. It was wrapped in a skirt that night, with textured stockings underneath. When they reached his office, he clicked off his computer and went to get his coat from the back of his door. That's when he noticed Kat leaning onto his desk to look out the window.

"This is such a fantastic view," she said.

"Mm-hmm," Brunelle replied, not looking anywhere near the window. "It sure is."

Kat smiled at him over her shoulder but didn't move from her inviting position. In fact, she raised her skirt-wrapped ass just slightly.

Brunelle felt his pants tighten and recalled the lock on his door. In a moment, the door was locked and his coat was strewn across a guest chair. He pressed himself against her and she pushed back, lowering her head and moaning ever so softly. A few seconds later, her skirt was pushed up and his pants were pushed down, and he slid easily inside her. It didn't take him long—he'd been aroused for some time before her arrival, and it was supposed to be a quickie anyway. For her part, Kat made that low groan she always did when he entered her, but otherwise kept remarkably quiet while he thrust in and out of her. He came with a low grunt of his own and kissed her between her shoulder blades. Then, almost as quickly as they'd dropped, his pants were back up, her skirt was back down, and he was holding her on his lap as they both looked out the window at the fantastic view.

She nestled against his chest and sighed. He kissed the top of her head and wished he hadn't been thinking of Robyn the whole time.

CHAPTER 20

The next week, Brunelle walked into Perry's courtroom and was greeted by a smiling Jessica Edwards.

"Good morning, Dave," she chirped from where she was organizing her papers for the hearing. "Did you have a good weekend?"

Her frustration from losing the competency hearing had apparently dissipated. That was par for the course for the good trial attorneys. You had to care enough to be angry when you lost, but smart enough to get over it so you could move on to the next battle. Brunelle would have been equally pissed if he'd lost. As it was, he got to gloat and celebrate up in his office.

"Meh," he replied. "It was okay."

Edwards looked up from her stuff. "Only okay? What's the matter, trouble at home?"

Brunelle grimaced. He didn't mind having an official girlfriend, but he bristled at the box it put him into.

"No trouble," he insisted. "In fact, we went to the museum. Saw an exhibit by some guy named Ravensclaw."

Edwards laughed. "Rauschenburg," she corrected. "I heard that's supposed to be a great exhibit."

"Meh," Brunelle repeated as he set his own things onto his table.

"Not a big art fan?"

"I think I'm an art fan," Brunelle replied. "I'm just not sure it was art. It looked like painting after painting of brown rocks."

"Spoken like a true troglodyte," Edwards chided. "Open your mind a bit. Try something new. You never know what you might like."

Brunelle nodded. He'd been thinking the same thing, although not about art. "I guess. But I can think of better ways to spend four hours."

"Four hours?" Edwards exclaimed. "It took you four hours?"

Brunelle nodded and grimaced. "There were a lot of rocks."

He left out the argument he'd had with Kat during the third hour when she'd had enough of his sarcastic wisecracks about the rocks. She'd reminded him they were there for Lizzy, which just pissed him off more because she was right and he felt bad about being a jerk. So he'd pouted for the last hour. Not his finest moment. Or four hours.

The secure side door to the courtroom clanked and swung open. Two corrections officers escorted Keesha Sawyer into the courtroom from the jail and directed her to the seat next to Edwards. The attorneys broke off their chit-chat and Edwards started trying to explain to Keesha what they were doing that morning. She seemed to understand and Brunelle wondered if she was getting tired of being talked to like she was stupid, rather than mentally ill.

A few minutes later, Perry took the bench, storming out of his chambers and barely giving his bailiff a chance to call out the obligatory, "All rise!"

Brunelle looked around the courtroom and found himself disappointed that Robyn wasn't there. She was probably back in Presiding, actually doing her job.

"Good morning, Your Honor," Brunelle stood up and began to make the record. "We're here today for a status conference. I was thinking that we could first select a trial date, then discuss what steps need to be taken in advance of the trial."

"You don't need to tell me what we're here for, Mr. Brunelle," Perry snapped. "I'm not that old yet. I remember. And we're not going to set a trial date first. The trial date will depend on what needs to be done to prepare for trial, not the other way around."

He turned to Edwards. "The first thing I want to know is what the defense is going to be. Ms. Edwards, will you be endorsing an insanity defense?"

Brunelle sat down again. Perry had a point. And he was interested to see if losing the competency hearing had changed Edwards' mind about the desirability of an insanity defense.

"No, Your Honor." Edwards stood up to address the court. "We will not be endorsing insanity. We will be pursuing diminished capacity."

Brunelle shook his head. That was a dead bang loser for Edwards. They both know it. So did Perry.

"Diminished capacity?" he scoffed. "You're going to claim she didn't intend to kill her mother?"

"I'm going to show," Edwards replied, chin raised, "that her mental illness prevented her from forming the requisite intent for the crime of murder."

Perry narrowed his eyes. "How many times did she hit her mother with the hatchet?"

"That's not—" Edwards started.

"Twelve, I think," Keesha spoke up. "Maybe thirteen."

Everyone turned to stare at her. One of the many surreal things about criminal proceedings was that the defendant—the one who had the most at stake—rarely spoke. He or she was supposed to sit there and listen, like a potted plant, while everyone else discussed them and made decisions affecting the rest of their lives.

Brunelle suppressed a smile, then looked to the court reporter. He raised an eyebrow to ask whether she'd gotten Ms. Sawyer's comment. A quick nod from the reporter confirmed it. He'd have to remember to order a copy of the transcript. 'Everything you say can and will be used against you'—including spontaneous outbursts in court.

Edwards bent down and admonished her client to stay quiet. Keesha nodded amicably. She seemed like a nice enough homicidal maniac.

"That's not the point," Edwards returned to her argument. "The State has to show that she intended to commit a crime. She intended to defend herself and others. That's not a crime."

Brunelle shook his head. "The State only has to prove that she intended to commit the act she did. That it wasn't an accident. We don't have to prove she was trying to break the law."

"Says you," Edwards retorted.

Brunelle was taken aback by the juvenile response. He smiled but before he could think of a response, Perry took control again.

"Fine. There will be no insanity defense. The defense is diminished capacity. You'll need expert testimony as to her mental state at the time of the offense. Has she been evaluated for that yet?"

"Er, no," Edwards answered. "We fully expected to win the competency hearing, so we didn't have Dr. Adrianos address that in his evaluation. We'll be contacting him shortly to—"

"No," Perry said. "I'm appointing the expert to conduct the evaluation. You're not bringing in that Dr. Atlantic again."

"But, Your Honor," Edwards argued. "I believe we can select our own—"

"No," the judge interrupted. "You can't. You've endorsed your defense, now I'm appointing the expert to conduct the mental exam. Mr. Brunelle, what was the name of your expert again?"

Brunelle was surprised by the question, but ready to answer it. "Uh, Thompson, Your Honor. Dr. Gregory Thompson."

"Right." Perry turned back to look down at Edwards. "Thompson's your doctor. He'll conduct the evaluation."

"But he's the State's expert." Edwards protested.

"He's the *court's* expert," Perry declared. "And he will conduct the examination. One exam. You will both be present and he will file his report directly with the court."

The judge paused just long enough to see if he was going to get any more push-back from Edwards, but she seemed lost in her thoughts. Or, more likely, her anger.

"The trial will commence one month from today," he announced. "Do you have any scheduling problems with that, Mr. Brunelle?"

Brunelle knew the right answer. "No, Your Honor."

The judge didn't ask Edwards.

"We will have another status conference in two weeks," he went on. "The mental examination will be completed by then or the defendant will be precluded from claiming diminished capacity. Is that clear, Ms. Edwards?"

"Crystal," she growled through gritted teeth.

"Good." Perry banged his gavel. "Court is adjourned."

Once the judge had closed the door to his chambers,

Brunelle stepped over to the defense table. "I like being in front of a judge who listens to the lawyers, don't you?"

Edwards glared at him. "Fuck you, Dave."

Brunelle knew not to take it personally. Instead, he offered to help. "You want me to contact Thompson to schedule the exam?"

Edwards opened her mouth to say something, probably caustic judging by the expression on her face. But then a smile suddenly appeared. "Yeah. Sure. Thanks, Dave."

Brunelle smiled back. "No problem. What are opposing counsel for?"

He'd mistaken her smile for resignation.

CHAPTER 21

Thompson's evaluation of Keesha was scheduled for the following Wednesday, in the jail. The following Wednesday, because that was the first day Thompson was available. In the jail, because Perry wasn't about to sign an order transporting her out to Western State Hospital again.

Chen would also be there, as lead investigator and for extra security, not that they'd likely need it. But still, he would be able to document the interview and testify to anything Keesha might say regarding the incident. He and Brunelle met Thompson in the lobby of the jail. It was a spartan affair: cinderblock walls, linoleum floors, and one corrections officer behind bulletproof glass. There was a row of small lockers for visitors' cell phones and valuables, and a single, heavily armored door into the jail, controlled by the aforementioned corrections officer.

The officer was a large man, an impression exaggerated by the bulletproof vest beneath his uniform. The three men exchanged their department IDs for visitor badges and Chen grabbed a locker for their things.

As Brunelle pulled out his phone, he noticed his message light flashing. He touched the screen and muttered, "Oh, great."

"What is it?" Chen asked.

Thompson ignored their conversation and slid his own phone into the locker.

"Oh, nothing." Brunelle realized he shouldn't have said anything. "It's just Kat. She texted me. A few times."

"Everything okay?" Chen inquired.

Brunelle laughed. "Oh, yes." He held up the phone. "I'm not making this up: she wants me to pick up some milk on the way home."

Chen laughed. "Wow. I didn't know you guys were married."

"We're not," Brunelle was quick to reply.

Chen waited a moment, then pointed out, "You didn't say 'yet.'"

"No," Brunelle agreed as he slipped his phone into the locker. "I didn't."

Chen closed the locker and gave the corrections officer a thumbs-up. He buzzed the door open and Brunelle and Thompson followed Chen through a series of locked doors and barred gates until they reached the jail's multipurpose room. The inmates were allowed to use it for things like playing board games and holding Bible studies. It was the only room large enough to fit everyone invited: Brunelle, Chen, Thompson, Edwards, Keesha, another corrections officer, and—to Brunelle's private delight—Robyn Dunn.

She smiled when she saw Brunelle notice her, flaunting that dimple at him, but she didn't say anything.

So he did.

"Are you going to have co-counsel after all, Jess?"

Edwards shook her head as she set her notepads and pens on the room's only table. "No, Robyn's just here to observe. I told her what we were doing today and she begged to come along."

Brunelle raised an eyebrow at the young redhead. "Is that right?"

"I'm very good at begging," she assured with a wink.

Brunelle closed his eye momentarily to chase away the impure thoughts flooding his mind. When he opened them, he noticed Chen staring at him with an obvious 'What the hell?' look. He pretended not to notice.

"You ready to go, Larry?"

Chen nodded slowly, looking to Robyn, then back at Brunelle again. "Yeah. I think we better get this done quick."

Thompson was already settling in. The long table had been placed in the center of the room. Keesha was sitting at one end of it. To her left sat Edwards, then Robyn. To her right was Thompson. Brunelle sat next to Thompson and Chen sat at the other end, directly opposite Keesha. The guard stayed standing, against the cinderblock wall, a few feet directly behind Keesha.

"Hello again, Keesha," Thompson started.

"Hello, Dr. Thompson," she replied pleasantly.

Brunelle noticed Keesha had her hands folded calmly on the table. He noticed it because they weren't cuffed. But then he remembered that both Chen and the corrections officer had holstered firearms and forearms the size of Keesha's leg. He told himself to relax.

"Let's start with the night in question," Thompson said. "Do you recall what you were doing before you went to bed?"

"My client," Edwards announced, "will not be answering any questions about the alleged crime."

Brunelle dropped the pen he'd gotten out to take notes. "Jess, it's a dim cap eval. She has to answer questions about the crime. He's trying to determine her state of mind at the time of the murder."

Edwards shrugged. "My client has the right to remain silent," she insisted, "and she is asserting that right."

Keesha looked like she was more than ready to discuss the killing, but she knew enough to follow her attorney's lead and stayed quiet.

"C'mon, Jess," Brunelle pressed. "You've done these before. You know how it works."

"Oh, I've done these before," Edwards agreed. "But never with the prosecutor and detective present. If she discusses the incident, then Detective Chen can testify as to what she said, regardless of Dr. Thompson's conclusion."

Brunelle ran a hand down his face. She had a point.

"Why is this different from you giving us a copy of the report afterwards?" Chen asked. "Either way we get a summary of what she said."

"The difference," Brunelle knew, "is that she doesn't give us a copy of the report unless she likes the results. If she had her own expert, this would all be secret and we'd only know about it if she intended on using the result at trial."

"That's bullshit," Chen said.

"That's fair," Edwards contradicted.

"That's the rule," Brunelle boiled it down pragmatically.

He realized Edwards was going to use this to go back in front of Perry and get an independent eval after all. He really didn't want to do that. He wanted to salvage the situation.

"Jess?" He stood up and gestured toward the corner. "Can we talk for a sec?"

Edwards stood up. "Of course, Dave," she smirked. She

knew she had him.

When they stepped away from the others, Brunelle started his pitch. "Look, I get what you're doing, but can't we work this out? My afternoon is shot anyway and Thompson came all the way up from Western State to do this. We both know he's going to say she didn't have diminished capacity, so let's just get it over with."

"That's why I'm doing this, Dave," Edwards replied. "It's bullshit that Perry ordered me to use *your* doc, then ordered that you get to sit in and write down everything she says. The only witness you'll have to call at trial will be Chen. He'll describe the scene, then recount whatever Keesha says today."

"Don't forget her confession at the hospital," Brunelle joked.

"Oh, I haven't," Edwards replied. "Which is exactly why I can't let her talk to you again."

Brunelle looked over at the table. Keesha was still sitting there quietly, looking up at the ceiling. Thompson was looking down at his notes. Robyn was looking over at him. She smiled again.

Chen was just sitting there, arms crossed, and not really looking at anything.

"Hey, Larry," Brunelle called out. "Come over here for a second."

He had an idea.

When Chen stepped up to them, Brunelle made a proposal. "What if we agree that anything Keesha says here can't be used against her in my case-in-chief? Chen won't testify about this at all. Just the stuff at the house and at the hospital. The only way it comes in is if she takes the stand and testifies contrary to what she says here today."

Edwards hesitated. That meant he had a chance. He pressed his advantage.

"We do it all the time with snitches," he reminded her. "They give us the info first, to convince us they have shit on their codefendants. If it's good, we use them. If not, we don't. But we agree up front, anything they say can't be used against them personally. That encourages them to be honest."

Edwards shook her. "And they usually still lie."

Brunelle smiled. She was right.

"I don't know, Dave," she said. "Wouldn't that impact the eval somehow? She's not snitching to get a deal, she's getting a psych eval."

Brunelle frowned in thought. "Dr. Thompson?" he said. "Can you come over here for a moment?"

The psychologist looked up, then set down his pen and joined the powwow.

"What are we discussing?" he asked.

Brunelle never got to answer. It happened too fast.

In less than a moment, Keesha had Thompson's pen in one hand and Robyn's throat in the other. The guard was one step too far away. Brunelle and the others were even farther. Robyn barely had time to yell, "Jess!" before Keesha drove the pen into her face.

CHAPTER 22

What happened next was a blur. The guard was on Keesha in a flash, with Chen right behind. Within seconds, Keesha was on her stomach, handcuffed, with a mouth full of concrete floor.

Brunelle and Edwards went straight to Robyn. The pen had penetrated her left cheek, the butt of it sticking out just far enough to show that the point was several inches inside her mouth. Brunelle yanked it out and Robyn curled into a fetal position, hands covering her face as blood smeared the floor.

The medical staff burst in, called by the corrections officer's shoulder-mounted radio. They shoved Edwards and Brunelle out of the way. Robyn was whisked off to the jail infirmary and Keesha was dragged away by the team of guards who arrived right behind the medics.

Brunelle, Edwards, Thompson, and Chen were left standing there, shocked and awed by what had just transpired.

"Damn it, Jess," Brunelle lashed out. "This wouldn't have happened if you weren't playing games."

"Me?" she practically screamed back. "This is *your* fault.

Always trying to control everything and win at all costs."

Brunelle was about to fire back when Chen stepped between them. "Shut the fuck up," he ordered.

And they knew he was right.

CHAPTER 23

Judge Perry was appropriately horrified when he heard the news. Shaken, even. In a hastily convened hearing, he relented from his previous rulings, transforming from a pugnacious control freak into a passive handwringer. Edwards got exactly what she wanted. Adrianos would conduct an independent, and private, examination of the defendant. If he found diminished capacity—and of course he would—then Brunelle would be given his report. Thompson would be allowed to review and critique the report, but he would not do his own exam.

Brunelle didn't object to any of it. He was shaken too.

Back up in his office, he sat in his chair and gazed out the window, imaging the scenery over Robyn's red curls.

"Penny for your thoughts."

It was Chen, standing in his doorway.

Brunelle forced a smile. "I'm a lawyer, Larry. Those thoughts start at two hundred bucks an hour."

Brunelle abandoned his window and Chen took a seat. "What brings you by?" Brunelle asked.

Chen jabbed a thumb toward the hallway. "I just dropped off my report on the pen-stabbing with Nicole. I figured you'd want to look at it as soon as possible."

Brunelle nodded. "Did you write it up as Assault in the First Degree?"

"Naw, I went with Attempted Murder. You pull that shit inside the jail, in front of a cop and a guard—I'm writing that up as high as I can."

Brunelle nodded, understanding the detective's point.

"You gonna charge it Attempted Murder," Chen asked, "or wimp out with Assault One?"

"I'm not gonna charge it all," Brunelle replied. "At least not now. I charge her up now and Jessica becomes a witness. That means my murder trial gets derailed. She'll get pulled off the case and we'll have to start all over with a new defense attorney. No, I'll wait until the murder trial is over, then charge her up. Statute of limitations is three years. I've got time."

"You're the boss," Chen said. He grinned. "I'd say you knew what you were doing, but I know better."

Before Brunelle could respond, Nicole walked in with a manila folder. "I opened a new file on Sawyer's assault of that public defender." She handed it to him, then looked at him appraisingly. She set a hand on his shoulder. "You okay?"

Brunelle reached up and laid his hand on hers. "Yeah," he insisted. "Just a little shaken. I feel kind of responsible for what happened."

"Nonsense," Nicole replied. "You're not responsible for what some crazy woman does."

Brunelle shrugged. "I hope Robyn agrees."

Nicole squeezed his shoulder. "I'm sure she does."

Brunelle managed a lopsided smile. He removed his hand

from his secretary's and tapped the file. "I'm going to hold off filing charges until after the murder case is over," he told her.

"Oh, okay," she said. She started to reach for the file, hand still on his shoulder, resulting in her lowering her chest right in front of his face.

Brunelle looked up at her. "No, leave the file with me. I'll just stick it inside the murder file for now."

Nicole straightened up and headed for the door. Brunelle's eyes followed her. She turned when she reached the door frame. "Let me know if I can do anything for you, David."

"I will," Brunelle replied. Thanks."

Once she'd left, Chen leaned forward in his chair. "What the hell was that?"

The question jarred Brunelle. "What the hell was what?"

"I thought you and Kat were serious."

"We are serious," Brunelle defended. "I mean, we haven't talked about moving in together or getting married or anything, but yeah, we're serious. I think."

"Then stop flirting with everything in a skirt," Chen admonished.

Brunelle felt affronted. "I wasn't flirting," he insisted.

"Okay then." Chen pushed back in his seat and crossed his arms. "Stop staring at every set of tits you see."

"I wasn't staring at Nicole's—" Brunelle stopped himself before he said 'tits.' It seemed demeaning to her. "I wasn't staring at her."

"And you weren't flirting with that young defense attorney either," Chen challenged. "The pen-holder."

"Wow," Brunelle half laughed. "Pen-holder? That's just cold."

"And you're just fooling yourself," Chen replied. Then he leaned forward again and rested an arm on Brunelle's desk. "Look,

Dave. It's perfectly normal. You've been single all your life. Now you've finally met someone you're serious about and it's a little scary. It's natural for you to want to confirm you still have it, even if you're about to give it up."

Brunelle lowered his eyebrows. "What am I giving up?"

Chen ignored the question and pulled out his phone. "I know just the thing," he said as he starting typing. "I was talking with the wife about you the other night and she agreed."

"Agreed about what?" Brunelle asked. Then, "Wait. You talk about me?"

Chen looked up with a grin. "Of course."

Brunelle was flummoxed. "What do you say? And what did your wife agree about?"

"She agreed," Chen replied, "that you're scared of commitment because you don't understand the benefits of commitment."

"I am not scared of commitment," Brunelle protested.

Chen raised an incredulous eyebrow. "Sure. Anyway, now you're going to see the good side of commitment."

Brunelle was suspicious. "Oh yeah?"

Chen hesitated for a moment as he read the responsive text he was getting. "Yeah. And confirmed."

Suspicious turned to anxiety. "What's confirmed?"

"Our double date. You and Kat and me and Evie."

Brunelle's jaw dropped.

"This Saturday," Chen went on gleefully. "Dinner and a movie."

Brunelle just shook his head. "Wow. A double date."

"Excited?"

"I think," Brunelle said, still shaking his head, "I'd rather have a pen shoved through my cheek."

Chen laughed. "I know someone who could help you with that."

Brunelle regretted the joke, even though he appreciated Chen's quick-witted reply. He looked down, a thousand thoughts rushing through his head, not the least of which were Kat bent over his desk and Robyn bleeding on the floor.

"Cheer up, Davey. It'll be fun," Chen said. Then he winked. "Maybe you'll even get lucky."

CHAPTER 24

"Miss Dunn is in room E-397," said the station nurse on the third floor of Seattle's Swedish Hospital. "But visiting hours are almost over."

Brunelle glanced at his watch. He had ten minutes. He didn't suppose it would take longer than that. "Thanks. I'll be quick."

The room was at the end of the hallway, past several other rooms filled with the sounds of television game shows and loud telephone conversations. When he reached E-397, he found Robyn sitting up in her hospital bed, a blue and white hospital gown draped over her frame and a book on her lap.

She had a large bandage over the left half of her face.

"Knock, knock," Brunelle said as he stepped into the room. He suddenly felt awkward and wished he'd brought a card or flowers or something.

Robyn looked up from her book. "Mr. B." She smiled—as much as the bandage would allow. "Wow. I didn't expect you to visit me."

Brunelle wasn't sure what to say. He supposed maybe she

was right. So he avoided the topic. "How are you feeling?"

Robyn slid the book aside. Brunelle spied the spine: James Joyce. He was impressed, although really, he didn't know enough about Joyce to know why he should be.

"Not bad," Robyn answered. She hovered a hand over the dressing. "It still hurts, but the doctors said I can go home tomorrow."

"Well, that's good," Brunelle remarked.

Robyn nodded. "Yeah. I think they're just keeping me an extra night 'cause I work for the county and our insurance is so awesome. Good thing I have a medical fetish."

Brunelle smiled nervously. "I never know when you're kidding."

"No, really," she winked. "We have great insurance."

Brunelle shook his head. Then he looked closely at her face. "I forget which side your dimple is on. I hope it survived intact."

Robyn smiled broadly. The dimple was on the other cheek. "You noticed my dimple?"

Brunelle nodded. "Yeah. It's very endearing."

"I always hated it," Robyn confessed. "How lame is it to have a dimple on only one side?"

"I kinda liked the asymmetry," Brunelle said.

Robyn laughed. "Well, sorry. Now I'll have a scar on the other side to balance it out."

Brunelle frowned. "Sorry about that."

"It's okay," Robyn said. "It'll match the scars on the inside."

Brunelle's frown deepened. "You're too young to have scars on the inside."

Robyn surrendered a quiet, dark laugh. "I started young."

Brunelle regarded her for a moment. "There's a lot more to you than just some pretty young attorney, isn't there?"

Robyn smiled again. "You think I'm pretty?"

Brunelle felt himself start to blush. But he didn't mind this time. "Well, I hear you think I'm dashing."

Robyn's smile twisted into a frown. "I never said that. Peter's a liar."

"If you never said it," Brunelle grinned, "how did you know I heard it from Peter?"

The frown wavered, then transformed into that dimpled smile again. "You're good," she said. "You should be a lawyer or something."

Brunelle laughed. "Yeah. I'll look into that."

They were quiet for a few moments, but again Brunelle didn't mind it.

"Thanks for pulling the pen out of my face," Robyn finally said.

"The least I could do," Brunelle answered. "Although I'm not sure it was the right thing to do, medically speaking."

"No, I'm pretty sure it's okay to extract writing instruments driven into someone's face by a crazy person. It's a rule or something."

"She is nuts," Brunelle agreed. "Are you angry at her?"

Robyn sighed. "Of course I am. I could say I'm not, but I am. I'm going to have a scar on my face for the rest of my life. So yeah, I'm angry. But I'll get over it."

"Will you?"

"I've gotten over worse."

"Does it matter to you that's she's crazy?"

"We're all crazy, David." Robyn meet his gaze earnestly. "Every one of us. Some of us are just more functional than the rest. The key is finding the right person. Someone who fits the crazy instead of making it worse."

"Sounds like you've thought about it a lot."

She shrugged and looked down. "I suppose. Thinking about it doesn't always help though. I know why I fall hard for older men in authority positions, but it doesn't make it feel any less intense."

Brunelle thought he might understand the intensity. "So what do you do?"

"Hope," she answered, looking back up at him. "Hope that you fall for a guy who doesn't hurt you. For that older man in the authority position with the quick wit and the steely gaze, and maybe this time he's also a nice guy. One who'll accept you, and protect you, and not add to the scars. Maybe even help the scars heal."

"Scars don't heal," Brunelle pointed out. "That's why they're scars."

Robyn closed her eyes and sighed. "I know."

And visiting hours were over.

CHAPTER 25

Even though the double date was several days after his visit to the hospital, Brunelle still carried the conversation around with him. That was his first mistake.

He also couldn't stop thinking about the Sawyer case. He had a tendency to do that—fixate on a case as it came up for trial. That was his second mistake.

And he hadn't told Kat about Keesha's attack on Robyn. He didn't want to talk about Robyn to Kat—at least not until whatever infatuation he was feeling had faded a bit. So he just avoided any mention of her. Which meant not telling his girlfriend about one of the most memorable things ever to happen in front of him. That was his third mistake.

Finally, Chen had selected the latest Hollywood romantic comedy for their date movie. It starred some young leading man all the women could pretend they were with, and the latest starlet all the men could wish they'd been with. That wasn't a mistake, but it put him in a bad mood. The worst mistake of all.

Evie Chen waited for her husband to take a bite then jumped in where he'd left off.

"So that's why we always stay on the Big Island when we go to Hawaii."

"Sounds wonderful," Kat remarked.

Brunelle was lost in his own thoughts. He stared down at his steak and rice pilaf. Kat reached over from her seat next to him and took his hand. "We should go to Hawaii sometime," she said.

"Uh, yeah," Brunelle knew to agree. "That sounds nice."

Kat squeezed his hand. He had to admit, he liked how her hand looked in his. It was a lot smaller. It fit just right.

"You okay?" she asked.

"Hm? Oh, yeah. I'm fine. Just preoccupied, I guess."

"Still thinking about the stabbing?" Chen guessed.

"What stabbing?" Kat asked.

Fuck, thought Brunelle. He knew the double date had been a bad idea.

"Didn't he tell you?" Evie said. "Larry said it was pretty gruesome."

"No." Kat smacked Brunelle's arm playfully. "He didn't tell me anything. What happened?"

"I didn't tell you?" Brunelle feigned surprise. "Sorry. It must have slipped my mind."

"How does that slip your mind?" Chen asked. "She had a pen sticking out of her face."

"A pen?" Kat gasped. She grabbed her boyfriend by his shirt. "What the hell happened?"

So Brunelle told the story. Actually Chen jumped in and told most of it, Brunelle offering the occasional comment along the way.

"So it was jutting out of her face?" Kat asked even as she put a forkful of food into her mouth.

Brunelle shrugged. "Yeah. It was pretty nasty."

"Davey here was the hero," Evie said. "He pulled it right out. Got a face full of blood for his trouble."

"You did?" Kat asked.

Brunelle shook his head. "No blood spurt out or anything, but it was kind of all over the place. And Larry was the hero. He smashed that bitch into the floor. I'm more the goat. If I hadn't called everyone into the corner, she never would have gotten the chance."

Kat squeezed his hand again. "Don't be silly. She's responsible for her own actions. Well, kind of. I mean, she's crazy, right? So there's no way to know what she might do."

"Kind of my point," Brunelle responded.

"Well, I'm the cop," Chen offered. "It's more on me than you. And it's really on that corrections officer. He never should have let it happen."

Brunelle shrugged. "Still…" he protested weakly.

"Well, if you feel so bad," Kat said, pulling her hand back to continue eating, "maybe you should go visit her in the hospital or something."

Brunelle froze. *Fuck.*

He could agree and leave it at that. Or he could admit that he already had visited her. Nothing wrong with that, right? In fact, she'd just suggested it, so it must be okay. On the other hand, it was different to do it after she'd suggested it than to do it beforehand and not mention it at all. She'd hear about it eventually anyway. But maybe if he shut up right then, by the time she heard about it, she might think it happened after her suggestion. Then again, if he didn't admit to it right then, in response to a very specific suggestion, and then she figured out he'd already gone, well, that would be the worst possible result. She'd know he had kept it from her intentionally. He had nothing to be ashamed of, except for his feelings and motivations. Ironically, keeping quiet just then was the most likely way to expose them.

He cut off a piece of steak. "Actually, I already did," he tried to say casually, then stuck the food in his mouth.

Everyone's eyebrows raised. "You did?" Chen asked.

"You didn't mention that earlier," Kat observed. She was grinning, but it was more Cheshire Cat than happy Kat.

"I think," Evie said as she pushed away from the table, "I'm going to use the restroom." She looked at her husband. "Maybe you should go too," she more than suggested.

Chen was obviously familiar with his wife's tone. "Yes, dear." He stood up and looked down at Brunelle. "Good luck."

Once they'd left, Brunelle glanced sideways at Kat. "Was it something we said?" he tried to joke.

"I think it was something you didn't say," Kat replied. She was still talking between bites. Brunelle thought that was probably a good thing. If she were really angry, she'd have her utensils down. Or at his throat.

"Why didn't you tell me about the stabbing?" she asked.

Brunelle shrugged. He decided to keep eating too. It gave him something to look at besides Kat. "I guess I just forgot."

"Did you forget to tell me you visited her too?"

"I guess so. Sorry."

Kat shook her head and thought for a few moments while she chewed another bite.

"She's cute, isn't she?" she asked without looking at him.

"Not any more," Brunelle deadpanned.

"Nice," Kat laughed. "I forgot how sensitive you can be."

Brunelle ventured a grin. "Part of my charm."

"Is that why you didn't tell me?" Kat pressed. "Because you

thought I'd be jealous?"

Brunelle shrugged again and took another bite. They were sitting next to each other, so it was awkward to look at her. "I dunno. Maybe. I guess I just don't always tell you everything that happens to me."

Kat nodded for a few seconds. She took another bite and washed it down with a sip of wine. Then she reached out and turned his chin toward her. "Relax, David. I'm not looking to get married again. Not any time soon anyway. And maybe not to you. Who knows? Larry thought this would be fun. He said you'd been stressed out lately. I noticed it too. You have a stressful job. Seeing a young woman get attacked like that doesn't help. I don't want to add to that stress. We'll go to Hawaii or we won't. We'll spend Christmas together or we won't. We'll end up an old married couple or we won't. But relax. We'll take it at our own pace and it'll work out or it won't."

"I want it to work out," he said. This time it was him who took her hand.

"I know." Kat smiled. "Me too. So relax and let it. Otherwise you're going to have a nervous breakdown."

Brunelle laughed. "I've spent enough time with psychologists and crazy people lately."

"Then let's chill out so you don't get involuntarily committed."

"I'm all for that," he quickly agreed.

Then Kat got an evil grin. "Wanna have some fun?"

Brunelle looked around. "What? Right now? Here?"

Kat smacked him again. "Not that, Romeo. Geez. There'll be time for that later. No, when Larry and Evie get back, let's pretend like we just had a huge fight."

"Ooh, that's not very nice."

"I have a nasty streak too, David," Kat seemed proud to say. "Let's play a little. No reason you should be the only one going crazy."

CHAPTER 26

"Is he fucking crazy?"

Brunelle threw his hands in the air when Duncan delivered the news. "Fargas is suing us? Us? The prosecutor's office?"

"He's suing everybody," Duncan confirmed. "Us. The jail. Western State. Even the drug company that made her anti-psychotics. Everybody."

"Everybody with a deep pocket," Brunelle clarified. "When did this happen?"

"This morning," Duncan answered. "He filed the complaint as soon as the clerk's office opened."

"The trial starts next week," Brunelle complained. "He couldn't wait one fucking week?"

"Civil thinks the timing is intentional," Duncan said. "To box you in."

'Civil' meant the civil division of the prosecutor's office. The largest and most high profile division was the criminal division. Brunelle had spent his entire career in the criminal division. But the office was also the law firm for all of the county's agencies, giving legal advice and, when necessary, defending against lawsuits filed against the county. The lawyers over there were a different breed from criminal prosecutors like Brunelle, but they were all on the same team.

"How does this box me in?" Brunelle asked. "It pisses me off. One week before I start picking a jury and the news is going to be filled with how this woman is crazy and everyone in the world except her is responsible for the murder of her mother. Yeah, that pisses me off, but I don't see how it boxes me in."

Duncan sat down in his desk chair and motioned Brunelle to sit opposite him. "Well, it's like this. Fargas' theory of liability is that Western State never should have released her because she was dangerous."

"Obviously," Brunelle answered. "He shouldn't have too much trouble proving that."

"Exactly," Duncan agreed. "So that's why they're suing Western State. But remember why she was there. She committed a robbery that we dismissed."

"We had to dismiss," Brunelle protested. "Western State said she was incompetent."

"And you, good sir, just proved she's not any more. Congratulations. So, Fargas is alleging that we should have refiled the robbery charges when she was released. If we had, she would have been in jail instead of at home hacking her mother to bits."

"Are you fucking kidding me?" Brunelle slapped his forehead. "The grapes case? That would have been pled down to a shoplift and she would have gotten credit for time served. She would have been out on the street either way."

"You and I know that," Duncan agreed. "And Fargas does too, I'd wager. But the standard range sentence on a Robbery One is three years in prison. If we'd refiled and convicted as charged, then she would have been in prison."

Brunelle pinched the bridge of his nose. "So, because I won the competency hearing, we're being sued?"

Duncan shrugged. "We were probably going to get sued either way. But yes, that helped. Way to go."

Brunelle frowned, shaking his head. "Okay. Fine. But I don't see how I'm boxed in."

"Did you notice who isn't being sued?" Duncan asked Socratically.

"I haven't seen the actual complaint," Brunelle pointed out. "Did he leave someone out?"

"He's only suing the government agencies, not the individual doctors. Or," he pointed at Brunelle, "prosecutors."

"Me?" Brunelle laughed darkly. "I don't have deep pockets. I work for the government. Besides, I have immunity for things I do as a prosecutor."

"Only if those things are ethical," Duncan said,

"What the hell does that mean?" Brunelle snapped.

"It means that if, say, you intentionally lost the case to undercut Fargas' lawsuit against the prosecutor's office, then he could sue you personally."

Brunelle sat up straight. "I would never do that."

"Of course not," Duncan agreed. "And Fargas knows that too. Probably. But by filing his lawsuit before you begin your trial, if you lose, he can claim you did it on purpose. It insulates his lawsuit from an acquittal in your case."

Brunelle ran a hand over his head. "Fuck. Matt, she's nuts. I may very well lose this case no matter how hard I try."

"I know." Duncan nodded. "So get ready to get sued if you do."

Brunelle looked at his shoes and shook his head. "Could this get any worse?"

"I'm afraid so," Duncan said.

Brunelle looked up at him. Duncan frowned. "If you lose, to protect the office, Civil says we might have to fire you."

Brunelle stared at his boss for several seconds. Then he lowered his head into his hands. "Well, fuck."

CHAPTER 27

The Readiness Hearing was the Friday afternoon before trial. Not all of the judges still held them, but Perry did. He was a control freak after all. As the name suggested, it was the time for the attorneys to confirm they were ready for trial. Perry took the bench promptly at one o'clock.

He started with Edwards.

"Is the defense ready for trial?" he asked.

"Yes, Your Honor," Edwards rose to respond.

"And are you still pursuing a diminished capacity defense?"

"Yes, Your Honor."

Perry frowned. "I've read all the reports. Ms. Edwards. Despite what I said earlier, I'll give you one last chance. Are you absolutely certain you don't want to seek a verdict of not guilty by reason of insanity?"

"Quite certain, Your Honor," Edwards replied. "Thank you."

Perry sighed and shook his head. He turned to Brunelle.

"Are you ready to get started, Mr. Brunelle?"

Brunelle considered the last few weeks. Echoes of the judge's question bounced around inside his mind, each taking on a different voice.

Are you ready to get started? Perry had asked.

Are you ready to get beat? Edwards' voice taunted him.

Are you ready to get sued? Fargas asked.

Are you ready to get fired? Duncan asked.

Are you ready to get serious? Kat asked.

Are you ready to get married? Chen asked.

Are you ready to get crazy? Robyn asked.

"Yes," Brunelle answered. "I'm ready."

CHAPTER 28

Jury selection took too long. Too many people had heard too much about Fargas' damned lawsuit. The ones who knew a lot or had strong opinions about it were excused for cause. The ones who insisted they could be fair despite their obvious bias were bounced by the attorneys using one of the six peremptory challenges each side got. The folks who were left made up the jury—like the old joke about no one wanting to be judged by twelve people too stupid to get out of jury duty.

The whole process had taken almost two days. It was late on Tuesday afternoon when the jury was sworn in. Too late in the day to fit in both Brunelle's and Edwards' opening statements, so Perry adjourned early and directed everyone to return first thing in the morning. That would give the attorneys time to fine tune their presentations, and the media time to arrive and set up. Jury selection was boring. But opening statements in the case with the crazy woman who murdered her mother because she was turning her into a zombie and she never should have been released from the nut house in the first place? That was going to lead the news.

As Brunelle approached the entrance to the courtroom the next morning, he passed a row of reporters wearing headsets and bent over laptops connected by cables to the single 'pool camera' Perry had allowed inside. Brunelle knew most of them and nodded as he went by. Inside, he recognized a few more reporters in the first row and spied the pool camera in the back corner, already aimed at where he and Edwards would stand to deliver their openings.

He set his things down on the prosecutor's table and caught Edwards' eye. They nodded to each other but didn't say anything—like former college teammates now on different pro teams. All friendship and respect before the game, but no mercy once the whistle blew. She was already settled in, her client having been brought in the secure side door well before anyone could see her in cuffs. She was dressed in regular street clothes too. Jurors weren't allowed to see that a defendant was being held in custody prior to trial. It might prejudice their verdict if they knew the judge thought the defendant was too dangerous to walk the streets. So these jurors would hear about a paranoid schizophrenic who hacked her own mother's face off with a hatchet, but be expected to believe she was out on her own recognizance. And the three armed corrections officers stationed right behind her and at each exit were just extra bailiffs. No, really.

Brunelle scanned the gallery for familiar faces. He knew he wouldn't see Kat or Chen; they were witnesses and witnesses had to remain outside the courtroom until they testified. The only exception would be Thompson and Adrianos, who'd be allowed to hear each other's testimony but no one else's.

Duncan was in the first row, along with a couple other prosecutors Brunelle knew. Similarly, a few of the public defenders had stopped by to hear the openings before returning to the Pit. He knew Nicole wouldn't be there; the secretaries actually had work to do. And Fargas was in the second row, next his clients, arms crossed and a frown under that stupid moustache.

But the one face Brunelle was hoping to see wasn't there.

Probably just as well, he told himself.

Perry took the bench at the stroke of nine. After confirming with the lawyers there were no issues to be taken up before openings, the real bailiff led the jurors out of the deliberation room. Just as they finished filing into the jury box and sat down, the door to the hallway opened one last time and in slipped a young red-headed defense attorney who took a spot standing in the back.

Brunelle made eye contact with her. She stuck one finger in her dimple and the other in the mottled scar on her opposite cheek, just below her eye. Then, with a huge grin and slight curtsy, she twisted both fingers like Shirley Temple.

"Ladies and gentlemen of the jury," Perry boomed. "Please give your attention to Mr. Brunelle who will deliver the opening statement on behalf of the prosecution."

Brunelle stood up, straightened his suit coat, and faced the jury.

Showtime.

CHAPTER 29

"When I was in third grade," Brunelle began his opening statement to the jury, cameras rolling, friends and colleagues in the gallery, a woman's life hanging in the balance, "I stole a candy bar."

Not what anyone expected for an opening statement on a murder case. *Good.* He had their attention.

"It was called a 'Powerhouse.' I don't think they even make those any more. It had a blue wrapper, I remember that. And I remember exactly how that rack of candy bars looked that day. The Powerhouses were on the bottom, to the left. I can still see my hand reaching out for that damn candy bar.

"I didn't really want to steal that candy bar. I mean, I liked Powerhouses a lot. And I'm pretty sure I ate it afterwards. But it wasn't like I didn't have the money, or my parents wouldn't let me eat candy at home, or anything like that. No, I could have bought it and eaten it and everything would have been fine. That's what I should have done, if it was about eating the candy. But it wasn't. It was about stealing. I stole the candy bar so I could steal something. That's what I was trying to do.

"I was with some friends that day. That's pretty much why I did it. They dared me, so I did it. I don't even remember who they were. They weren't good friends. They weren't the kids I think of when I look back on grade school and remember my friends. It wasn't Zack or Craig. It wasn't Scott or Bobby or Jamie. It was just whoever I was hanging out with that particular week, or month, or season. And they were probably good enough kids too. None of us were starving or being beaten at home by parents who thought candy was evil. We were just kids, but we were growing up.

"And there wasn't anything particular about the store, except that's where we were when they dared me to steal a candy bar. It was just some drug store downtown. In fact, it was worse. It was actually a Bible store, and they kept a rack of candy at the front for the kids. The only reason we went in there was because they had some cool-looking erasers in the shapes of alien spaceships. I'm pretty sure we paid for those. But I stole the candy bar."

Brunelle stopped and took a small sip of water. He could use the moisture on his throat, and it was a natural transition point in his story.

"I never got caught. There was no dramatic scene where the storekeeper chased us out into the street, or grabbed me by the arm until the cops came and my dad let me sweat it out down at the station. Nope. I got away with it. I ate the candy bar. And I never got in trouble. I don't think I ever even told my parents. But of all the things I've forgotten over the years—and I've forgotten a lot— I've never forgotten that moment when I went against what I knew was right and made the decision to do something wrong."

He paused, putting his hands together in front of him and taking on a thoughtful tone. "I think the reason I remember it so vividly isn't because it was the first time I did something wrong. I'd done plenty wrong before, and I've done wrong since. I'm sure I'll do something wrong in the future too."

He resisted the urge to glance at Robyn.

"No, the reason I remember it is because it was the first time I really decided to do something wrong on purpose. I could have blamed it on my friends. They put me up to it, after all. And I'm sure I would have done that if I'd gotten caught. But since I didn't get caught, I didn't have to defend it. I didn't have to make excuses or blame others. I was left with my own responsibility. And not having had to deny it externally, I had no choice but to accept it internally."

Another pause and another sip of water. He set the cup on his table and stepped back in front of the jury to begin the next section of his opening.

"One way to look at life and growing up, is how we make decisions, and how we accept the consequences of our decisions. When we're infants, we don't get to make the decisions. We can cry when we're hungry, but the parents decide when we get fed, when our diapers get changed, when we go down for a nap. When we're children, we get to give more input, but the decision is still our parents'. We don't declare what we're going to do, we ask if we can. Can I watch TV? Can I have another cookie? Can I stay up late tonight? But each time, it's the parent who says yes or no. The fact that the child even asks the question shows they don't even think about having the decision-making power.

"Then we're teenagers, and we rebel. Or not. Some of us did, some of us didn't. Some of us did it hugely, dramatically. Some of us did it quietly, secretly. But this is when we think we're making the decisions, but we're not quite there yet. We may be making the decisions, but we aren't feeling the full brunt of the consequences. Our parents are still there to bail us out. Our teachers and guidance counselors forgive us and try to get us to see things straight before it's too late.

"And that's when you know you're really an adult. When it's too late. When not only do you get to *make* decisions, but you get to live with them. When your decisions hurt other people and it's not all right and it won't be okay again. When you own your actions and all of the consequences that go with them. You don't ask to be fed. You don't ask to watch TV. You don't ask for the keys to the car. You make a decision. And if you screw it up, then you live with the consequences."

Brunelle lowered his gaze and nodded. "I think that's why I still remember stealing that candy bar. I didn't get any consequences from that. No one knew about it except for a few dumb kids who weren't my friends the next year anyway. But deep inside, I knew I had made a decision to do something wrong. My friends didn't make the decision. The devil didn't make me do it. I did it. I thought about it. I planned it. I weighed the pros and cons. Then I did it. Me. And whether there were real life consequences or not, I was responsible for that decision. I still am."

He looked up again.

"In the early hours of August twenty-eighth, Keesha Sawyer got up out of her bed in the basement of her mother's house. She went to the garage and got the hatchet they kept there with the other yard tools. She went upstairs to her mother's bedroom and went inside. She stood over her mother and looked down at her sleeping. Then she raised her arm and drove the blade of the hatchet into her mother's face."

Some of the jurors flinched. *Good.*

"She pulled the hatchet out of her mother's face and swung another blow. Again and again. Every time she did, blood and pieces of flesh flew off the blade and stuck to the bedroom walls. You're going to hear testimony from the medical examiner who performed the autopsy in this case. She's done literally thousands of autopsies, and hundreds involved what doctors call 'sharp force trauma.' Her job is to look at the injuries on a body and tell you exactly what happened. How many injuries, in what order, and what they did to kill the person. She's going to tell you that she doesn't know how many times Keesha hit her mother's face with that axe-blade, because there wasn't enough of her face left to know."

The jurors looked repulsed. *Perfect.* Time to wrap it up.

"Ladies and gentleman, I submit to you that this is both an easy case and a hard case. It's an easy case because there will be no real disagreement about what happened. This isn't a whodunit. Keesha done it. It's not an episode of C.S.I. There aren't exotic scientific tests that helped crack the case. The facts aren't in dispute. When this trial is over, you will know exactly what happened. That's what will make it easy.

"But it's a hard case too because even though you will know that Keesha Sawyer murdered her mother, you're not going to want to convict her. You see, Keesha Sawyer is mentally ill. She hears voices and she has paranoid delusions. She thought her mother was turning her into a zombie, and all the kids in the neighborhood too. She thought she had to kill her mother."

Brunelle saw the wave of indecision ripple through the jury box. That was the defense, and it was a good one. He needed to kill it in the crib, so to speak.

"She was wrong."

It was as simple as that.

"Decisions have consequences. Even when we're wrong." He paused and raised a finger for emphasis. "*Especially* when we're wrong. Keesha Sawyer may be mentally ill, but she's capable of making decisions. She's responsible for those decisions. She killed her mother. She was wrong to do so. And at the end of this trial I'm going to stand up and ask you to find her guilty of Murder in the First Degree. Thank you."

Brunelle sat down at his table and looked up at the judge. He wanted to look at the jurors, but he knew better. He could ask Duncan later how they received it. He also wanted to look at Robyn, but he really knew better. He could ask her later what she thought of it. Most of all, he also wanted to look at Edwards, to see if he'd shaken her at all. But it would look smarmy and challenging. He'd know in a moment.

"Now, ladies and gentlemen," Perry said, "please give your attention to Ms. Edwards who will deliver opening statement on behalf of the defendant."

CHAPTER 30

Edwards stood up slowly and thanked the judge. Then she stepped into the attorney well—the area between the counsel tables, the witness stand, the jury box, and the bench—and faced the jury. One more moment of silence to make sure everyone was looking at her.

Except Brunelle. He was taking notes. He'd need to know what she promised so he could remind the jurors what she failed to deliver. And if he stopped and just listened, it would look like he was as enraptured by her advocacy as she hoped the jurors would be. Confident disinterest was the proper affect, just in case any of the jurors looked his way.

"Good morning, ladies and gentlemen," she began. "Thank you for your service and thank you for your attention. This is a case about how the system is broken. And how it failed not just my client, but my client's mother."

Great, Brunelle thought. *Did Fargas write this?*

In any event, he was happy to go down that road. It could be the system's fault too for letting Keesha go, but that didn't wash the blood—and bits of flesh—from her hands.

"Mr. Brunelle just told you a moving story about a youthful transgression of his, and I'll return to that in a bit, but I'd like to start with the most important thing he said. You can tell it was important, because he barely mentioned it. He just stuck it in toward the end, kind of sandwiched between his walk down memory lane and the actual point he was trying to make. And that most important thing is this: Keesha Sawyer is mentally ill.

"There will be no disagreement about that in this trial. You will hear from not one, but two different psychologists who will tell you that she suffers from paranoid schizophrenia. Now, contrary to what you see on TV, schizophrenia does not mean multiple personalities. That's a different disorder. Schizophrenia is when you hear voices in your head, and you see things that aren't there, and you have paranoid delusions that people are out to get you. It's organic, it's debilitating, it's incurable. And it's a living hell.

"Keesha's symptom started when she was a teenager. Voices and thoughts she couldn't control, taking over her mind. Her parents didn't have a lot of resources, so she didn't get the help she needed. She self-medicated with alcohol and street drugs, but that only made things worse. Only made the symptoms accelerate. Only made her lose her mind that much faster.

"She started getting into trouble with the law. Small things at first. Shoplifting and scuffles. Disorderly conduct. Shouting at the voices when she was waiting for a bus. Prostituting herself to get money for the drugs that made the voices quieter for a few hours. And then one day, tired and hungry, she stole some grapes from a grocery store. That's theft. When the security guard grabbed her, she punched him. And that shoplift became a robbery. She was arrested and charged with her first felony. But instead of being prosecuted, she was committed to Western State Hospital so she could be treated for her schizophrenia.

"This time, the drugs helped. They weren't street drugs. They were prescription pharmaceuticals, dosed and administered by trained mental health professionals. She got better. Not perfect. Not like you and me. But better. And they sent her home."

Edwards paused. She stepped back to her table, but instead of picking up a cup of water like Brunelle had, she picked up a red and orange neck scarf. It didn't match her dark suit and white blouse at all. She draped it loosely over her neck and continued her presentation.

"Mr. Brunelle told you that Keesha killed her mother. That's correct. She did. There will be no argument from us about that. She absolutely did it, and she did it pretty much the way Mr. Brunelle described. But ladies and gentleman, that's not the whole story.

"Mr. Brunelle said she did it and that's that, and she's guilty of murder and that's that. But, ladies and gentlemen, that is not that, because you will need to find that Keesha intended to do what she did, and you will hear from Dr. Peter Adrianos, the director of Cascade Mental Hospital, who will tell you that Keesha couldn't have formed that intent because of her schizophrenia."

Brunelle frowned. Edwards had steered directly from statement into argument. Opening statements were supposed to orient the jury about what they were going to hear. Arguing any specific legal conclusions from that evidence was argumentative and objectionable. But Brunelle didn't object much, especially during openings. The judge was unlikely to sustain it, Edwards was unlikely to change her script, and the jury was guaranteed to be annoyed. So he kept taking notes and tried not to look concerned.

"Mental illness can be a difficult thing to truly understand. You and I know there are no such things as witches and zombies, but for people like Keesha, they don't know that. In fact, they might believe it just as strongly as you and I believe the sky is blue. So rather than tell you what Keesha thought and look at this case from the outside, I'd like to try something. I'd like us all to enter her world, and look at this case from the inside."

She grabbed the ends of the scarf. "When I tie this around my neck, we will enter Keesha's world. Whatever she believes will be the truth, and we'll try to understand the case through her eyes."

Brunelle had to look up for this. It was one thing to casually take notes. It was another to completely ignore what he had to admit was a pretty good parlor trick. He'd have to remember this one and figure out if he could use it himself somewhere down the road.

Edwards tied the scarf, then looked up at the jury, her eyes a little too wide, her shoulders set off just a little strangely.

"Keesha Sawyer was released from Western State Hospital to the custody of her mother, the woman who raised her from a babe. The woman who took care of her as a young child and tried to tell her right from wrong. But Keesha remembered how, when she was sixteen, the angels came and warned her about her mother. They spoke directly into her mind so her mother couldn't hear. They told her the truth. They were angels. They wouldn't lie. Her mother was a witch, and she couldn't be trusted. No one could be trusted. Except the angels. Thank God for the angels."

Brunelle forced himself to look down again. Edwards was doing a damn good job of creeping everyone out. He'd gotten sucked in too.

"The angels were quieter at the hospital. They were still there. They were always there. They were her friends. Her only friends. The only ones who would never leave her. Sometimes they were mean. Sometimes they yelled. But they never abandoned her. And they never lied. Never.

"When she got home, the voices got louder. The doctors said that might happen if she didn't take her pills every day, but it was hard to remember. And the voices needed to get louder. Because she was home again. With her mother. The witch. She loved her mother. She was supposed to. But the angels didn't love her mother. And the angels were always right. Always.

"Then it started happening. She didn't know about it at first because she was asleep when it happened, but the angels told her. They told her that every night when she went to sleep, her mother would kill her and turn her into a zombie. She didn't want to be a zombie."

Edwards tugged at her scarf. "Remember: zombies are real. *Real.* And so are witches and angels. These are all as real as birds in the sky or worms in the ground."

Nice touch, Brunelle thought. *Worms in the ground. Nice and icky. Like this story.*

"So when the angels told Keesha that her witch mother was killing her in her sleep and turning her into a zombie, Keesha didn't know what to do. The angels couldn't stop it. All they could do was talk. Talk and talk and yell and talk. It was up to her. But what could she do? It was her mother. She was a witch. And she was her *mother.* So just like she always did, she suffered and hoped and cried and wished it would all just stop. But she didn't *do* anything.

"Until the angels told her about the children."

Edwards paused. Brunelle looked up. The whole damn jury was on the edge of their seats. *Fuck.* He looked down again.

"Her witch mother had started killing the neighborhood children too. She was turning them into zombies too. She couldn't let that happen. The angels told her and they wanted her to do something. She never would have done it to save herself. But she had to save the children. Because otherwise," again Edwards tugged on her scarf, "those innocent children would be murdered by a witch and turned into zombies. For real."

Edwards stopped again. She slowly undid the scarf and balled it into her fist. She looked straight at the jury. "And then Keesha Sawyer did exactly what Mr. Brunelle said she did. Only now, you know why."

Edwards turned and dropped the scarf on her table, right in front of Keesha, a brilliant maneuver to make the jurors look at her very real client instead of ignoring her like the formality of a criminal trial tends to suggest everyone do. She stepped back in front of the jury and delivered the *coup de grace*.

"Mr. Brunelle told you when he was nine, he stole a candy bar, but never got caught. But what he left out was that if he had been caught, he wouldn't have been prosecuted. He was too young. He would have been sent home to be grounded. And even if he had been charged, it would have been in juvenile court, not adult court. The juvenile system is separate because it's about education and rehabilitation. He would have taken a couple of classes and written a letter of apology. He would have learned his lesson and it would have been over and that would have been the right way to handle it.

"You treat kids differently because they don't understand like adults do. You treat the mentally ill differently for the very same reason.

"Keesha Sawyer is not guilty of murder.

"Thank you."

Edwards sat down.

Touché, thought Brunelle. The battle was joined.

CHAPTER 31

"The State may call its first witness," Perry announced.

The choice of first witness was always an interesting one. There were different theories about how best to lead off a homicide case. Some prosecutors always began with a member of the victim's family, to remind the jury that a real live person was dead. Some prosecutors always started off with a neutral witness—a bystander or passerby—someone who could just tell the jury what happened without being cross examined about their biases. Some prosecutors always started with the first cop on scene, to give the case a 'whodunit' feel, and get the jury invested in the investigation.

Brunelle had learned over the years that every case was different and to listen to the case. It would tell him who to call first. For the Sawyer case, the decision was easy. Often, the main parts of a case had to be broken up over several witnesses, which could be confusing to a jury. But in this case, there was one person who responded to the scene, observed the body, and heard the confession.

"The State calls Detective Lawrence Chen."

The judge swore Chen in and Brunelle quickly laid down the introductory stuff. Larry Chen. Seattle P.D. Detective. Nearly thirty years on the force. Fifteen as a detective. Ten in major crimes.

"Were you on duty in the early hours of August twenty-eighth?"

"I was on call," Chen corrected, turning to deliver his answer to the jury, not Brunelle, like they'd taught him three decades earlier at the academy. "I wasn't on the clock. I was home sleeping. But if I was needed, I'd get a call."

"Did you get a call?" Brunelle stood almost behind the jurors, at the very end of the jury box, to make sure even the last juror could hear the witness, just like they'd taught him two decades earlier in law school.

"I sure did," Chen answered.

"What kind of call?" Brunelle didn't have a script of questions. Just a legal pad he left on his counsel table with a bullet-point list of the information he needed to elicit. He could form a question on his feet; it was the answer that mattered. So when he was done, he'd double check his list, make sure he hadn't missed anything, then sit down with a confident, 'No further questions.'

"It was a homicide call," Chen said.

Brunelle nodded. Everyone in the courtroom knew it was a homicide call. He and Edwards had just said as much. But he had to lay the story out, one step at a time. He led Chen through the drive over to the house, parking in front of the house, and walking up to the porch steps.

"What happened when you reached the front door?"

Chen turned and looked at Keesha. "The defendant opened the door and let us in."

"Did she say anything?"

"She said, 'That was quick. I just called you guys.'"

"So Ms. Sawyer called 9-1-1?"

"Yes," Chen answered. "I didn't realize at first that she was the one who had murdered the victim. Initially I thought she was the first person to find the body. That's who usually calls 9-1-1."

"Not the killer?"

"Not the killer," Chen confirmed.

"When did you realize she was the one who had killed the victim?"

"Not until after she showed us the body," Chen said. "Or, what was left of it."

Brunelle nodded. Before he asked his next batch of questions, he took a stack of photographs from the bar. They had already been pre-marked by the bailiff. Edwards had objected to them pretrial as too gruesome. Perry had overruled the objection. Sometimes the truth was gruesome.

"I'm handing you a series of photographs, Detective," Brunelle said for the record as he did so. "Do you recognize what's depicted in those photos?"

Chen nodded as he slowly thumbed through them. "Yes. This is what I saw when I went up to the bedroom."

Brunelle took the photos back and stepped over to the overhead projector set up between the counsel tables. There was a projection screen on the far wall. The jury would have to look past Keesha to see the screen. That is, Brunelle knew, when the jurors saw what he was about to show them, they'd see Keesha too.

He placed the first of the photos on the projector. With a push of a button, the image would be displayed three feet high for all the world to see.

"Before I show these to the jury," Brunelle turned back to Chen, "this was a very disturbing scene, wasn't it?"

Chen frowned as he considered the question. He turned

again to the jurors. "There was a lot of blood," he said. "A lot. All over the bed and the floor and the walls. I've seen that kind of thing before though. What made it so bad was the condition of the victim's body. Her face."

"How did you react to it?"

Chen grimaced. "I've seen a lot in my career. I've learned to ignore the smell and look for clues."

"Were there other officers there with you?"

Chen offered a crooked smile to the jury. "Yes. At first. A couple of young patrol guys."

"How did they react?"

"One guy was okay. The other went outside and threw up."

Brunelle pressed the button.

The first photo actually wasn't all that bad, if you didn't know what you were looking at. It was a wide shot of the whole bedroom. Without knowing to look on the bed, you might not even have noticed the body in the middle of the blood-soaked sheets.

Brunelle walked up to Chen and handed him a laser pointer. He wanted the jury to know where to look.

They went through the photos, each one moving in systematically until they finished with a close-up of was left of Georgia Sawyer's face.

Most of the jurors had looked away more than once as Brunelle had progressed through the pictures. By the end, though, they were all managing to look at the image across the room. Just above Keesha Sawyer's head. They may have been repulsed, but they were also transfixed. *Good.*

"Detective, you said you've seen a lot in your thirty years of experience, is that right?"

Chen nodded. "Yes."

"Have you ever seen anything quite like this?"

Chen thought for a moment, then shook his head. He turned to the jurors. "No."

Without looking at his legal pad, Brunelle mentally checked off Part I of his direct examination: The Scene. Time for Part II: The Confession.

"You said earlier that Ms. Sawyer admitted to killing her mother after you'd seen the body. Where did that conversation take place?"

"In her living room," Chen explained. "We all sat down and she got some cookies for us."

"Did you eat any?"

Chen grimaced again. "No. Not after what I'd just seen."

A few of the jurors nodded sympathetically. *Good.* that meant they liked Chen. Jurors usually did. The best detectives weren't the hard-asses; they were the big, lovable teddy bears. Teddy bears with guns.

Brunelle nodded. He glanced over at Keesha, so the jury would too. "What did Ms. Sawyer say?"

"I asked her when she found the body, but she said she didn't understand," Chen related. "I thought maybe she was in shock from what she'd seen. So I clarified, asking her what time did she go upstairs and see that her mother was dead. She kind of smiled and said, 'No, officer. When I went upstairs, my mother was still alive.' That's when I got it. She had blood on her clothes, but I had thought that was from trying to render aid or embrace the body. Then I realized it was cast-off."

"What's cast-off?"

Chen looked to the jury to explain. "When you extract a weapon from a body, the force of pulling it back will cause the blood on it to fly backward off the blade. It gets on the walls and, often, the killer. Usually it's fine lines of droplets, but she had so much, it blotched like she'd actually hugged the body."

"So what did you do?"

"We placed her in handcuffs and read her her rights."

"Did she agree to speak with you?"

"She insisted on it," Chen said.

Again he turned to address the jurors directly. "You know, it was strange. She was so calm. Not angry, not crying. Just calm. And even though she started justifying what she'd done, she wasn't defensive. Just very matter-of-fact. She told us her mother was a witch, she'd been turning people into zombies while they slept, so she had to kill her."

"Did you arrest her?"

"Yes, sir."

"Did you transport her to the jail?"

"No, sir."

"Why not?"

"Because," Chen told the jury, "she was obviously mentally ill. We took her directly to Harborview Hospital's emergency psych ward."

"What happened there?"

"The nurses administered intravenous anti-psychotic drugs."

Brunelle nodded. He remembered the next part himself. "Did that seem to help?"

Chen shrugged. "I guess so. I'm not a psychologist, but she said the voices in her head were quieter."

"Did you speak with her again after she'd been administered the drugs?"

"Definitely."

"Did her story change?"

Chen thought for a moment. "No. She provided more details, but the story was consistent. Her mother was a witch. She'd been killing Keesha in her sleep every night and turning her into a zombie. Then she started killing the neighborhood children and turning them into zombies too, so she decided she had to kill her mother."

Brunelle nodded. "That doesn't make a lot of sense, does it?"

Chen shrugged again. "It made sense to her. She'd thought about it, planned it, then carried it out."

Brunelle suppressed a smile. Chen had just summarized his entire case. A perfect ending to the direct exam.

A quick check of his legal pad, then, "No further questions."

Perry looked over to Edwards. "Any cross examination, counsel?"

"Yes, Your Honor," she replied, standing up.

She took her place at the bar, just a few feet from Chen. She had her notepad and a binder of police reports. She took a moment, organizing her materials, then looked up at Chen.

"Good morning, Detective," she started.

"Good morning," Chen replied.

"I'm not going to put that scene photo up again," she said, a subtle dig at Brunelle's motivations for having done so, "but do you recall how the scene looked that morning?"

"I'll never forget it, ma'am."

"I'm sure," she replied. "You said you've seen a lot in your career?"

Chen frowned to the jury. "Yes."

"And that was the worst thing you've ever seen?"

Chen's frown deepened. "It depends on how you define 'worst.' I've seen dead babies. I've seen bodies left out for weeks, half-liquefied and infested with insects. I've seen some seriously nasty stuff. I don't know if this was the absolute worst I've ever seen, but it was right up there."

Edwards nodded. "But this was different somehow, wasn't it?"

Chen thought for a moment. "Yes. I think that's fair."

"You've seen people who've been shot or stabbed or whatever, right?"

"Right."

"And usually, the injuries you see are basically just the ones that caused the death, right? Because once the victim is dead, the killer stops, right?"

Chen considered the question. "Yeah, I suppose that's true. You might have multiple gunshot wounds, but that's usually because the shooter fired multiple rounds at once, maybe a final kill shot, but nothing like this."

"This was different. This went beyond just killing the victim, didn't it?"

Chen nodded. "It seemed like it."

"In fact, Detective," Edwards said, "if there was just one word to describe what you saw in that bedroom that morning, that word would be 'crazy,' wouldn't it?"

Chen thought for a moment. "I'm not sure that would necessarily be the best word, but it would be a pretty good one."

"Crazy?" Edwards repeated.

"Yes," Chen agreed. "Crazy."

"No further questions," Edwards announced and she gathered up her things from the bar.

Brunelle waited a moment for her to sit down again, then stood up for his re-direct exam.

"Crazy?" he confirmed.

Chen smiled sheepishly. That word probably hadn't helped Brunelle's case any. He nodded. "Sure."

"But intentional, right?" Brunelle confirmed. "It wasn't

accidental?"

Chen's smile relaxed. "No, it wasn't accidental," he agreed heartily. "It would be hard to imagine anything more intentional."

That's better, Brunelle thought.

"No further questions."

Edwards passed on any re-cross and Chen stepped down from the witness stand.

Brunelle assessed the testimony in his head. Crazy but intentional. It felt like a draw. He hoped Kat would do better.

CHAPTER 32

"Dr. Kat Anderson," she identified herself in response to Brunelle's first question. "I'm an Assistant Medical Examiner with the King County Medical Examiner's Office."

"Did you conduct an autopsy on a person named Georgia Sawyer in relation to this case?"

"Yes."

Brunelle wanted to get right to the results, but he needed to educate the jury a little bit so when she gave her opinions, the jury would understand her—and trust her.

After extracting her education and experience, he moved on to the salient topic. "Could you explain to the jury what an autopsy consists of and what its purpose is?"

"Of course." Kat turned to the jury just like Chen. Professional witness. And a pretty damn cute one, too, he couldn't help but think.

"'Autopsy' is Latin for 'look for yourself.' The goal of an autopsy is to determine the manner and cause of death through forensic examination of the remains."

This next bit was important. "Could you explain the difference between *manner* and *cause* of death?"

Kat nodded. She'd done this before.

"Cause of death refers to the specific injuries or illnesses which caused the death. Manner of death refers to one of four broad categories that all deaths fall into, regardless of the specific mechanism."

"What are those four categories?"

"Homicide, suicide, accident, and natural causes."

Thank you, Brunelle thought. *We'll be coming back to that.*

"Okay," he said. "Let's talk about the cause of death first."

"All right," Kat replied. That wasn't the usual order of this kind of testimony, but then again this wasn't the usual case.

"Were you able to determine a cause of death?"

"Oh, yes," she told the jurors. "There was no doubt about the cause of death."

"What was the cause of death?"

"Sharp force trauma to the anterior head."

Brunelle figured he'd better have Kat translate that. "What is sharp force trauma?"

"Sharp force trauma occurs when a bladed or otherwise sharp object strikes the body, resulting in lacerations."

"Something sharp," Brunelle repeated. "Like a hatchet?"

Kat nodded. "Exactly."

"And what is the anterior part of the head?"

"Anterior means front," she translated. "The anterior head is the face."

"So sharp force trauma to the anterior head means...?"

"Someone struck her in the face repeatedly with a something sharp."

Brunelle knew this part was dragging a little long, but he

didn't mind giving the jury extra time to think about the type of weapon used, and the location of the injuries. Diminished capacity basically meant accidental. This was anything but.

"Can you determine what type of weapon was used based on the injuries?"

Kat thought for a moment. "Sometimes. The human body is elastic, so it's not like you can just match up a suspected weapon with an injury. But generally speaking, I can tell the difference between a knife slash, a knife stab, or say, an ice pick."

"What about the injuries here?"

"The injuries here," she told the jury, "were consistent with a broad-bladed weapon delivered with a great deal of force."

"A hatchet maybe?"

"Yes. I would guess this was a hatchet or small axe."

Time for more photos. And the jurors thought the scene ones were bad... These would be medical close-ups of Georgia's face. But they were necessary to fully explain Kat's testimony. She quickly identified the photos, taken over the course of the autopsy, and without apologies Brunelle put the first one up on the screen.

Several gasps escaped the jury box, and one choked sob. The gallery surrendered a few of its own gasps, followed by troubled whispers. Edwards looked impassively at the gore. Unfortunately for her, so did Keesha. Kat picked up the laser pointer and Brunelle asked his next question.

"Could you show the jury how you were able to determine that the weapon was most likely a hatchet?"

Kat nodded. "Of course."

So she explained it. Using the roving red dot, she pointed out the series of long lacerations, parallel and criss-crossing. She confirmed what everyone could see with their own eyes: the repeated blows resulted in sections of the flesh being completely severed. That allowed her to point out the fractures to the bone underneath. Which led to the next photo.

"Can you tell us what we're looking at here?" Brunelle asked, although he supposed everyone knew what a skull looked like.

"That," Kat answered, "is the skull, toward the end of the autopsy, after we peeled away the soft tissue. We needed to be able see the fractures up close. As you can see here, there are actually several deep cuts to the bone itself where the blade embedded itself before being pulled out again. You can also see the multiple fractures to the surrounding bone structures around the eye sockets and nasal cavity. In fact, several bone fragments were recovered elsewhere in the bedroom."

"What does that tell you?"

Kat paused. "Everything about this told me the same thing. The multiple strikes, the fractures, the extraction and cast off of soft tissue and bone fragments. They all told me that the killer drove the hatchet into the decedent's face repeatedly with tremendous force."

"How much force?"

"Enough to cleave bone."

"And how many times?"

Kat shook her head. She looked at the blown up photo of the broken skull. "I don't know. At least a dozen."

Brunelle nodded and turned off the projector. Two more areas, then sit down.

"Doctor, what are defensive wounds?"

Kat nodded and turned back to the jury. "Defensive wounds are injuries—usually to the hands and forearms—which indicate that the victim attempted to stop the attack."

"So, cuts to the palms from grabbing the blade," Brunelle got more specific, "or to the arms from blocking the blows?"

"Exactly."

"Did you locate any defensive wounds on Georgia Sawyer's body?"

Kat shook her head. "No. None."

"What does that tell you?"

"It tells me she didn't see the first blow coming, and the first blow was fatal."

Okay, last area. The one that mattered the most, given Edwards' defense.

"You said there are four manners of death?"

"Yes."

"And what are they again?"

"Homicide, suicide, accident, and natural causes."

Brunelle nodded. "Were you able to determine the manner of death in this case?"

"Oh, yes."

"What was the manner of death."

"It was clearly homicide," Kat confirmed what everyone knew. That wasn't the important part.

"Not accident?" *That* was the important part.

"Correct. Not accident."

"Thank you, doctor," Brunelle smiled at her, but managed not to wink. "No further questions."

He sat down, satisfied with how the direct exam had gone, but anxious about what Edwards might do. She was good. *Damn it.*

"You like movies, doctor?" Edwards started as she took her position at the bar.

"Movies?" Kat repeated, a bit taken aback. "Sure. I guess so."

"Do you like the classics?" Edwards went on. "Gone With the Wind? The Wizard of Oz?"

"I guess," Kat said. "I've seen those."

Edwards hesitated for a moment, a practiced pause. "It was

pretty messy when Dorothy threw the water on the Wicked Witch of the West, wasn't it?"

Brunelle shook his head slightly. *Really?* He peeked at the jurors to see if they were impressed. But he couldn't read their expressions. They were intent.

Kat smiled at the question. "Actually, as I recall, all that was left was her hat and robe."

Edwards nodded. "I suppose so," she allowed. "What about zombie movies?"

"Zombie movies?" Kat asked. "No, not really. I don't like gory movies."

Brunelle heard a couple of jurors chuckle at that bit of irony. *Good.* That meant they liked Kat.

He looked at her again. Yeah, she was pretty likeable.

Edwards elected not to be sidetracked by the irony. "Okay, but you're familiar with those types of movies and TV shows, right?"

Kat shrugged. "Sure. I guess so."

"So what happens," Edwards asked, "when the heroes shoot the zombie through the chest?"

"If I recall correctly," Kat qualified her answer, "the zombies keep coming."

"Exactly," Edwards replied. She stepped over to the projector but didn't turn it on yet. "Do you know how to stop a zombie?"

Kat frowned slightly, either in recollection or disgust. "I think you have to blow their heads off."

Edwards pressed the projector button and the image of the fractured skull reappeared on the wall. "Kind of like what happened here."

Kat pursed her lips as she considered. "I suppose so. Although I believe they usually use a shotgun in the movies."

Edwards turned off the projector again. "But those are just movies, right?"

"Right."

"Zombies aren't real, are they?"

"Not as far as I know," Kat answered.

"And anyone who believes zombies are real," Edwards asked, "they'd have to be crazy, right?"

Kat paused, her mouth twisted again in thought. "I don't know if they'd be crazy, but they'd be wrong."

Brunelle smiled. *Awesome. The perfect answer.* No wonder he liked her so much.

Edwards narrowed her eyes at Kat, but decided not to fight her. She'd made her point. "No further questions."

"Any re-direct, Mr. Brunelle?" Perry asked.

"No, Your Honor. The witness may be excused."

Kat had indeed done better than Chen. He hoped the rest of the trial would go as well.

CHAPTER 33

The rest of Brunelle's case-in-chief wasn't quite as interesting. It was a parade of patrol officers and forensic techs who processed the scene and collected the evidence. Somewhat dull, definitely repetitive, and unfortunately necessary. But he knew he needed to finish strong so he saved the most important for last.

"The State calls Dr. Gregory Thompson."

Thompson stepped up to the judge and got sworn in. As he took the stand, Brunelle turned and scanned the gallery for Adrianos. It was standard operating procedure for one expert to listen to the other expert's testimony, but Adrianos was nowhere to be seen.

The gallery had mostly cleared out over the course of the last few days. Openings were one thing. The testimony Police Officer Number 7 of 9 was another. Robyn hadn't been back since the openings, nor any of the other public defenders or prosecutors. The only things left from that first day of trial were the pool camera and Fargas. Fargas hadn't missed a day of the trial. He was probably billing his clients $300 an hour to sit his fat ass in the gallery and watch Brunelle do the heavy lifting.

Brunelle turned back to Thompson. Brunelle wondered if maybe Adrianos was just late. Could he really be so cocky that he didn't sit in on his rivals' testimony?

Thompson identified himself and gave his degrees and experience, then Brunelle got right to it.

"Are you familiar with the defendant, Keesha Sawyer?"

"Yes, I am," Thompson answered, nodding toward her.

"How?"

"I conducted a forensic mental health examination of the defendant."

"And how many such evaluations did you either conduct or review?"

That was the weak part of Thompson's testimony. He'd only done the one evaluation, and that had been about competency, not diminished capacity. His own attempt at a dim cap eval had been cancelled by the pen to the face. Perry's subsequent about-face had reduced Thompson's role to simply reviewing Adrianos' report.

"I conducted one exam myself," Thompson answered. "A second exam was aborted before it began. A third examination was conducted by another psychologist and I reviewed that report."

Okay. Brunelle shrugged inside. There was nothing he could do about it except lay out Thompson's opinions and wait for Adrianos' testimony. He knew the key to the whole case would be his cross of Adrianos.

No pressure.

"Before we discuss your conclusions, doctor, could you explain to the jury what is meant by the term 'diminished capacity'?"

Thompson nodded, but he didn't turn to the jurors to deliver his answer. The psychologists didn't testify nearly as often as the cops and when they did, it was usually in a pretrial hearing where there was no jury, just a judge.

"Diminished capacity," he told Brunelle directly, "refers to a psychological state where a defendant is incapable of forming the intent to commit a particular act."

Brunelle tried to get Thompson to engage the jurors. "That's a bit technical," he said. "Could you give the jury an example?"

Thompson nodded again, but ignored the twelve people to his right. "The easiest way to think about it is to realize that diminished capacity can also arise from intoxication, either alcohol or drugs. Not everyone has personal experience with the mentally ill, but most people have had experience with someone who's had too much to drink."

A couple of nods and a snicker from the jury box confirmed the jurors had such experience.

"So imagine," Thompson went on, "a man at a party who's had too much to drink. He's standing next to an attractive young woman he's just met. Then he grabs her somewhere inappropriate, say, her backside. Normally that would be an assault. But if he did it because he's so drunk he can barely stand and he just reached out for the nearest thing on instinct to steady himself, then he has diminished capacity as to the assault. He didn't intend to grab her there because his capacity to intend that was diminished by the alcohol.

"On the other hand, if the reason he grabbed her there was because the alcohol lowered his inhibitions and he intentionally did something he might not have done otherwise, well then, he still intended the act and he would be guilty of assault."

Brunelle smiled. That was a pretty damn good explanation.

"Have you formed an opinion as to whether Ms. Sawyer suffered from diminished capacity at the time that she killed her mother?"

"I have."

"What is that opinion based on?"

"It's based on my contact with the defendant, my review of the other psychologist's report, and my review of the evidence in the police reports, including the autopsy report."

"And what is your opinion?"

"It is my opinion that the defendant had the ability to form the intent to commit murder, and that she did intend to kill her mother when she struck her in the face multiple times with an axe. The defendant did not suffer from diminished capacity."

No need to check the legal pad. "No further questions."

Brunelle sat down and Edwards stood up for her cross exam.

"So my client intended to commit murder, is that your opinion?"

Thompson thought for a moment, careful to make sure he understood the question. "Yes, that's my opinion."

"Okay," Edwards said. "We'll get back to that."

Thompson shrugged, there being no actual question to respond to. Brunelle frowned. Edwards sounded way too confident.

"You've had the chance to personally examine my client for mental illness, correct?" she asked.

"That's correct."

"And your diagnosis was that she suffers from paranoid schizophrenia, correct?"

"Correct."

"That means she has paranoid delusions, correct?"

"Among other symptoms, yes."

Brunelle was impressed. Edwards was actually doing what lawyers were supposed to do on cross examination: lead, lead, lead.

Tell the witness the answer and make him agree. It was rude, but effective. And the tension made it that much more dramatic—and interesting—to the jury. He hoped Thompson would come through for him.

"And so the jury is clear," Edwards gestured toward the jury box without taking her eyes off her prey, "it's not that my client *claims* to hear voices. She actually does hear voices, correct?"

Thompson nodded. If he hadn't thought about looking at the jury during Brunelle's questions, there was no way he was going to now. He, like everyone else in the courtroom, was transfixed on Edwards. "Yes, that's correct. Auditory hallucinations appear very real to the person experiencing them."

"And similarly, she doesn't *claim* to think people are after her, she really does believe that, correct?"

"Correct."

"Her fear is real, correct?"

"Yes, the fear is real," Thompson agreed, "although the basis for it usually is not."

Edwards allowed herself a grin. "Yes, let's talk about that. There are no such things as witches, correct, doctor?"

"Correct," Thompson answered with his own smile. "Unless you count practitioners of the Wiccan faith."

Edwards nodded. "I mean old school, magic and toads and pointy hat witches. Those aren't real, are they?"

"No," Thompson agreed. "Those aren't real."

"And zombies aren't real either, correct?"

"Correct."

"But my client believes they are real, isn't that correct, doctor? Not just claims to believe they're real, but actually, truly, honestly believes they're real, correct?"

Thompson thought for a few seconds. "Your client

verbalized several delusions. I believe witches and zombies were some of them, yes."

"In fact," Edwards pressed, "didn't she state very specifically that she believed her mother was a witch and she was being turned into a zombie?"

Thompson nodded. "She did say that, yes."

"And she didn't just say that, she didn't just claim it, she actually believed it, didn't she, doctor?"

Thompson paused again as he considered his response. "Yes, I think that's true."

Edwards paused, tapping her chin and allowing Thompson's answers to sink in with the jury. "So, how do you kill a witch?" she asked.

Thompson's face showed his surprise at the question. "Uh, well, I don't know. Throw water on them?"

No laughter from the jury. They'd already heard the Wizard of Oz bit, and they could tell Edwards was on to something.

"People used to burn witches at the stake, didn't they?" she pressed.

"I think that's right," Thompson answered. "My area of expertise is psychology, not history, but that's my recollection from school."

"And that's because you can't just kill a witch the same way you kill a regular person, right?"

Thompson shrugged. "I'm not sure."

"Vampires need a stake through their hearts. Werewolves need a silver bullet. Right?"

Thompson shook his head. "I really don't know. I don't watch those kind of movies."

"What about zombies?" Edward asked. "You have to blow their heads off with a shotgun, don't you?"

Thompson was starting to bristle at the questioning. "You know, I can't really say. These are fictitious monsters, so I don't know if there really is a correct way to kill them. They're not real."

Edwards smiled and nodded. "They're real for my client, aren't they?"

Then Thompson seemed to understand. He nodded. "I suppose so," he admitted. "Yes."

Edwards nodded. She took a moment to review her notes, a signal to Brunelle that she was about to switch topics. He hoped she was almost done.

"My client didn't really have an accurate understanding of death, did she?"

Thompson frowned. "I'm not sure that's true."

"Well," Edwards said, "let me remind you. She said, did she not, that her mother was murdering her every night in her sleep?"

Thompson nodded. "Yes, she did say that."

"Yet she woke up every morning."

"She did."

"So when she said she was murdered every night, that wasn't accurate, was it?"

"No, it wasn't."

"But she believed it was true, didn't she? Because of her mental illness?"

Thompson paused to consider. "Yes," he said after a moment. "I think that's a fair statement."

"She thought it was possible," Edwards put it together for the jury, "for a person to be murdered and still wake up the next morning, isn't that true, doctor?"

Thompson shifted in his seat. Brunelle did too. "Yes," Thompson had to agree. "She did think that."

Edwards narrowed her eyes and pointed directly at him. "So

how can you say that my client—who truly believes her mother is a witch, who truly believes a witch needs more than a regular killing to actually die, who truly believes people can be murdered and wake up the next morning—how can you possibly say that she actually intended to kill her mother—for good, dead and gone, the way you and I think about death? How can you possibly say that?"

It was a long question, with too much information and too many subordinate clauses. But it was exactly the right question, artfully posed by a passionate advocate.

Thompson was boxed in. There was only one answer. He knew it. Brunelle knew it. And the jury knew it.

"How can you say that?" Edwards demanded.

"I can't say that," he admitted. "Not for certain."

Edwards had the knife in. She twisted it. "It's possible, isn't it doctor, that my client's intent was something less than murder? It's possible, isn't it doctor, that my client believed her mother would wake up the next morning? It's possible, isn't it, doctor, that my client believed this would get her mother to stop killing her too and all would be forgiven?"

Thompson frowned. He let out a sigh. "Yes. That's possible. All of that is possible."

Edwards stared at him for a moment. Brunelle looked back down at his notepad.

"No further questions," Edwards said.

"Any re-direct, Mr. Brunelle?" Perry asked.

"No, Your Honor," Brunelle replied, standing up. He decided to cut his losses rather than add to them. "The State rests."

And his case-in-chief ended not with a bang but with a whimper.

CHAPTER 34

Brunelle was walking down the hallway to the elevators when he heard a shout behind him.

"Brunelle!"

It was Fargas. Brunelle considered ignoring him and continuing toward the elevators. But he knew that wasn't the professional thing to do. And Fargas did represent the victim's family after all. *Damn it.*

He turned around to see Fargas waddling toward him. "Why, Mr. Fargas. What a pleasant surprise. Have you been watching some of the trial?"

"Fuck you, Brunelle," Fargas spat as he reached him. "You know I have. What the hell are you doing in there?"

Brunelle straightened up a bit. "I'm trying to hold a killer responsible."

"Well, you're doing a shitty job of it."

Brunelle kept the saccharine smile pasted on his face. "Thanks for noticing."

Fargas was turning red behind his moustache. "Are you

trying to lose? Is that it?"

Brunelle might have been offended if he hadn't already been briefed by Duncan. He knew Fargas was just trying to insulate his own case from an increasingly likely not guilty verdict. He didn't really believe Brunelle would throw the case. Probably. "I wouldn't do that."

Fargas frowned at him. "Because you're just so much better than anyone else."

Brunelle was a bit surprised by the comment. It seemed overly personal. "No, because I'm a prosecutor."

Fargas sneered at him. "No, you think you're better than lawyers like me. You have your cushy tax-payer funded salary and your guaranteed pension, while I have to be not just a damn good lawyer but an even better businessman. You wouldn't last two weeks in private practice, Brunelle."

Brunelle narrowed his eyes at Fargas, He didn't understand why Fargas was attacking him like that. He decided not to engage in the fight. He needed to keep his eye on the prize: convicting Keesha. "I don't know," he said.

Fargas' sneer unfurled into a rueful grin. "Well, you lose this case and I hear you may get to find out."

Subtle, Brunelle thought. He was done. "Goodbye, Mr. Fargas."

He turned and walked toward the elevators. Fargas muttered something after him. It was hard to hear, but it sounded like it rhymed with 'good luck.'

CHAPTER 35

"Cheer up, lover," Kat patted Brunelle's arm. It sent ripples into the glass of Jack Daniels in his hand. "I'm sure it went better than you think."

Brunelle frowned and took a sip of his drink. He didn't drink much, but when he did, it was whiskey.

"No, it didn't," he assured her. "You did great, but Chen said the scene looked 'crazy' and my doc admitted the defendant might not have had the requisite intent after all. I'm not sure how that could have been worse."

Kat faced forward again at the bar they were seated at. It was one of the popular after work spots in downtown Seattle. The restaurant section was full by the time they got there, so it was drinks and appetizers at the bar.

"Well, at least I did great." She took a sip of her wine. "That's what matters."

Brunelle surrendered a smile. "Of course. I'll be sure to lean on that memory when the jury acquits."

"You don't really think they'll acquit, do you?" Kat turned

back to him. "She's guilty."

Brunelle shrugged and took another sip of his drink. "I don't know. The problem is all these different legal standards for different mental health issues. Competency, diminished capacity, insanity. Each one has its own test, and they're all squishy."

"Yes, well," Kat cleared her throat. "I believe I've already mentioned I don't like squishy."

Brunelle nodded and smiled a bit. He wasn't really in the mood for it just then. "She might be insane, but I know she didn't have diminished capacity. I'm just not sure the jury will understand that."

"Well, that's your job to explain it, isn't it?"

Brunelle narrowed his eyes at his girlfriend. "Thanks. I know that."

She put a hand on his shoulder. "Relax, David. It's a hard case. You're doing your best. That's all that matters. What's the worse that can happen if you lose?"

Brunelle took a drink and set down his glass a little too hard. "She gets out and kills or hurts somebody else. Her family sues the prosecutor's office. To save face, they fire me. I end up homeless. Or worse, working for somebody like Fargas."

Kat grinned. "You forgot the locusts."

Brunelle nodded. "Right. And locusts. Thanks."

Kat looked him in the eye, holding his gaze for several seconds as an appraising smile danced across her lips. Then she looked to the bartender and raised her hand. "Check, please!"

"What are you doing?" Brunelle asked. "We haven't even ordered our food yet."

"We're leaving," Kat answered.

"Leaving? To where?"

"Your place."

Brunelle cocked his head at Kat. "Why?"

She leaned forward and kissed him on the lips. A long, hard kiss. "You need some stress relief," she purred.

Brunelle started to protest weakly. "You don't have to..."

Kat put some money on the bar, then stood up and took Brunelle's hand. "Of course I do." She pulled him off his barstool. "If I don't take care of you, someone else will."

CHAPTER 36

Adrianos was a complete asshole.

Brunelle kind of already knew that, but in case he'd had any doubts, all he had to do was listen to Edwards' direct exam. And, he insisted to himself, he wasn't just irritated that Robyn had skipped his entire case-in-chief but had suddenly popped up to watch Dr. Asshole's testimony.

What is it between those two? he wondered. Then he decided he didn't want to know. Not the details anyway. He decided to think about Kat and the previous night. After a few moments of pleasant memories, he realized he'd stopped listening to Adrianos.

Focus, Brunelle. Focus.

He looked up again at the psychologist. He was addressing the jury, turning toward them like Thompson never had.

"Mental illness is not very well understood," he was saying earnestly. "In fact, I would dare say only half of all psychologists truly understand it." He glanced playfully at Brunelle. "And none of the lawyers."

A couple of jurors laughed.

Yup, complete asshole.

"Why, doctor," Edwards feigned offense, "are you suggesting lawyers don't know everything?"

"What I would say," Adrianos turned back to the jurors, "is this. Lawyers know the law. The law attempts to address every aspect of our lives. Therefore, lawyers believe they know everything. In reality, they know how the law thinks the real world works, but often, they, and the law, are wrong."

Edwards nodded. "That's interesting," she said, as if she didn't know he was going to say exactly that. "Could you expound a little?"

"I'd be glad to."

Of course you would, Brunelle sneered. *More opportunity to talk.*

"We pass laws to address certain problems in our society," Adrianos posited. "And also to establish certain procedures. Often, the laws do little more than formalize what we already do as a society. For example, I suspect we began driving on the right side of the road before there was a law that required it. To the extent that laws reflect and reinforce our already existing customs, they hold a great deal of force.

"But there are other laws which lose their force as society moves away from the cultural norms which gave rise to them in the first place. Unfortunately, American history is full of such examples. Laws enforcing segregation, banning interracial marriage, excluding women from the vote. Indeed, many states still have laws which ban all but the most mundane sex acts, even between husband and wife. These laws may have reflected societal norms at the time they were passed, but society has evolved. All too often, however, the laws struggle to keep up."

"Are there examples of such outdated laws," Edwards asked,

sounding as canned as a sardine, "in the mental health field as well?"

"Yes," Adrianos assured the jury. "There are."

"Could you give us an example?"

Adrianos nodded. "I'll give you an example which pertains directly to this case. In this case, the government has accused Ms. Sawyer of murder. Now, to be guilty of murder, one must intend to kill the victim, and I will address in a moment how Ms. Sawyer does not possess the mental capacity to form such an intent. However, it will be useful to keep in mind that this idea of 'intent to kill' has also evolved over the years. Sometimes, the law doesn't change, but our interpretation of it does. Changes in the law require majority votes in the legislature and the signature of the governor. But changes in interpretation require only the reasoned application of evolved social mores to an existing legal standard."

Edwards interrupted. "Are you suggesting that judges or juries should ignore the law?"

"Oh, no," Adrianos assured.

Oh, no. Of course not, Brunelle thought sarcastically.

"What I'm suggesting," the psychologist said, "is that our legal standards are made up of words, and the meaning of those words will necessarily change over time."

He looked again to the jurors. "Let me give you an example. It was once the case that if a man came home to find his wife in bed with another man, he could very intentionally kill his wife but only face a conviction for manslaughter. There was a court-created doctrine of 'hot blood' that essentially lowered the severity of the crime from murder to manslaughter based on a widely held societal belief that a man in that situation would be both understandably distraught and justifiably homicidal. There was never any statute which authorized the murder of a cheating spouse, but that was how the law was applied for over a century.

"In the last couple of decades however, the doctrine of 'hot blood' manslaughter has quietly gone the way of segregation and exclusively male suffrage. Not because the law of murder has changed in any way; it hasn't. But because we, as a society, have changed our view of such killings. Feminism and the rise of women's rights have had a direct effect on the way the murder statute has been interpreted. It used to be, the men in the town who were the policemen and lawyers and judges and jurors, would say to the killer, 'Joe, I understand why you did that.' Now, the men *and women* who make up those professions say to the killer, 'Joe, it doesn't matter. You can't do that.' And that change, I would say, is a good thing."

Brunelle had to hand it to Edwards and Adrianos. Not only were they doing a good job educating the jury, they were also setting him up to be a knuckle-dragging, racist, misogynist for daring to want to hold Keesha Sawyer responsible for her actions.

"So how does all this apply to whether Ms. Sawyer intended to murder her mother?" Edwards asked.

Adrianos smiled broadly. He was such an ass. "It applies because our understanding of the human mind has progressed light-years since the original legal standards for mentally ill defendants were established. Terms like 'competency' and 'insanity' and 'diminished capacity' are meaningless. No psychologist or psychiatrist would ever use such phrases. They're like leeching and bleeding to a modern physician. The only people still categorizing the mentally that way are lawyers, applying standards they don't understand, from an era they'd never want to go back to. Don't ask a lawyer if a mentally ill person is responsible for her actions. Ask a psychologist." He pointed at his chest. "Ask *this* psychologist."

And I'm the narcissist? Brunelle shook his head slightly.

"Okay," Edwards practically sang. "I'll ask you. Did Keesha Sawyer possess the requisite intent to commit the crime of murder?"

Adrianos listened intently, then turned to the jury. "No. She did not. Using the outdated legal terms you are saddled with, she suffered from diminished capacity."

"Can you explain how it can possibly be true that she didn't intend to kill her mother," Edwards asked, "when she struck her mother over a dozen times in the face with the blade of a hatchet?"

Adrianos nodded, his expression one of a soldier accepting his charge. "That's a very fair question. One any untrained mind might reasonably ask. But to a trained psychologist, the answer is simple. Keesha's subjective reality is also objectively real, at least to her. She didn't believe she would kill her mother because she didn't believe her mother could be killed. Accordingly, her intent could not have been to kill, for a person cannot intend to commit an act which she believes is impossible.

"In addition, to whatever extent she may have intended some form of harm to her mother, it was, for her, self defense. That is, she wasn't doing anything more than what her mother was doing to her, and accordingly, she was justified to do so."

"So she had no intent to kill?" Edwards parroted. "And it was self defense?"

"Precisely."

A lesser defense attorney would have stopped there, but unfortunately for Brunelle, Edwards didn't stop. She addressed the real concern the jury would really have back in the jury room once they began deliberations. "So what do we do with her? Do we just let her back out on the street so she can hurt someone else?"

"Let me answer your question with a question," Adrianos said. "Do we send an innocent person to prison just because we don't have anywhere else to put her?"

"No," Edwards nodded somberly. "No we don't."

She looked up at the judge. "No further questions."

Brunelle suppressed the urge to applaud. He may have found it rehearsed and trite, but Edwards had a point and there were likely several jurors who agreed with her. Or were willing to, contingent on how his cross exam went. This was the whole case. Brunelle knew it. He took a deep breath and stood up.

"Cross examination, Mr. Brunelle?" Perry asked.

"Yes, Your Honor," he replied. "Thank you."

He stepped forward and took a position one step too close to Adrianos. It acknowledged their adversarial position without being totally confrontational. He hoped it made Adrianos uncomfortable. He thought it probably didn't.

"So we apply the law if it leads to an acquittal," he started, "but we ignore it if it leads to a conviction, is that right?"

"Well twisted, counselor," Adrianos sneered. "But we both know that's not really what I said."

"Oh, I think you did." Brunelle replied. "Let's go through it. If the law says she's not guilty, we shouldn't convict her just to put her someplace safe. But the only reason the law allegedly says she's not guilty, is because you've interpreted a legal standard in a way that makes her not guilty, ignoring both the original intent and the plain language of that standard. That is, if the law says she *is* guilty, well then, the law is outdated and should be ignored."

"I never said we should ignore the law, counselor," Adrianos insisted. "I said we have to interpret legal standards like 'diminished capacity' using modern psychology, not the voodoo that passed for psychology back when these standards were first adopted by the courts."

"So under your interpretation," Brunelle pressed, "Keesha Sawyer suffered from diminished capacity when she killed her mother?"

"Under any interpretation that applies modern psychology," Adrianos refused to relent, "she had what you lawyers call diminished capacity."

Brunelle tapped the bar. He wasn't really getting anywhere. "You're very confident in your opinion."

Adrianos demurred. "I've had more direct interaction with Ms. Sawyer than any other doctor. Three in-person interviews, plus a full review of her mental health history, which, I can assure you, is quite extensive."

Brunelle frowned. Again, if only Perry hadn't cancelled Thompson's evaluation. If only Keesha hadn't used Robyn as a pen-holder.

"Well, yes, I suppose that's true. Although, it's routine for other doctors to review…"

Wait.

"Did you say *three* in-person examinations?"

"Yes," Adrianos confirmed. "Three."

Brunelle spun and looked at Edwards.

She whispered, "Fuck" and cinched her eyes shut. A split-second later she stood up and addressed the judge. "Your Honor, may we excuse the jury? I have a matter I need to raise outside their presence."

Perry glared down at her. There were few things a judge disliked more than having to shuttle an entire jury in and out of the courtroom during testimony. His expression suggested, 'Is this really necessary?' but his sigh showed that he knew it was. And why.

"Bailiff, escort our jury to the jury room, please. This may be an extended delay."

As the jurors rose and the bailiff carried out his orders,

Brunelle stepped over to Edwards' table. "Three?" he whispered.

"Shit, I'm sorry, Dave," Edwards whispered back. "I forgot to tell you. I had him meet with her again after Thompson's testimony. I meant to give you his report. I just forgot."

Brunelle sighed. It was irritating, but he knew it was true. Edwards didn't play dirty pool. They were all busy and in full-on trial mode. Sometimes things slipped your mind.

Perry waited for the jury room door to close, then turned directly to Edwards. "Do we have a discovery violation, counselor?"

Edwards hung her head. "Yes, Your Honor. It was an oversight. I just explained to Mr. Brunelle that Dr. Adrianos met with my client after Dr. Thompson's testimony. I meant to provide Mr. Brunelle with Dr. Adrianos' report, but forgot to do so until just now."

"Actually, I hadn't drafted a report yet, You—" Adrianos started to interrupt.

Perry still didn't like him. "Be quiet, Mr. Adrianos." He looked to Brunelle. "What do you want to do, Mr. Brunelle? Do you want a mistrial?"

A mistrial. Yes, he wanted a mistrial. The trial was going terribly for him. Kat was weak, Chen was weaker, and Thompson was the worst of all. Now Adrianos was the knight in shining lab coat, rescuing the world from medieval medicine. A do-over sounded great.

Except that the State never got a do-over. Mistrials granted on State's motions were automatically subject to double jeopardy review by the appellate courts. If Perry gave him a mistrial, odds were better than even that an appellate court would find that she'd already been tried once and he'd asked for the mistrial because the case was going so poorly. They'd dismiss the case out from under him before he ever got a second bite of the apple.

"No, Your Honor. I don't need a mistrial. But I need that report. And I think I should have it before I have to do any more cross examination of Dr. Adrianos."

Perry frowned, but nodded. He knew the dangers of a State-requested mistrial as well. He looked back to Edwards. "Can you get him the report tonight?"

Edwards looked to Adrianos. "Can you draft it by tonight?"

Adrianos nodded. "Absolutely. He can come to the hospital tonight and I will deliver it to him personally."

Brunelle bristled at having to go back to that asylum. Adrianos must have noticed the involuntary shudder.

"That way I can also show Mr. Brunelle the video of the interviews."

"Video?" Brunelle repeated. He turned to Edwards. "Did you know there was video? I never got any discs of video."

"We video everything," Adrianos explained. "But our system is proprietary. It can only be viewed on site, using our equipment."

When Brunelle hesitated, Adrianos assured him, "They're very short."

Brunelle sighed and turned to Edwards. "Wanna go to a movie tonight?" he joked.

She laughed lightly. "Sorry, Romeo, I have to wash my hair." She lowered her voice. "Besides, I'm done with my direct exam. I'm not going to that fucking nut house again. Especially not at night. Have fun."

"Great," Brunelle replied. Then he turned back to Adrianos and Perry. "Fine. I'll pick up the report and watch the videos tonight. Then I'll be ready to pick up my cross exam where I left off first thing in the morning."

Perry agreed to the plan. He looked at his bailiff. "Tell the jury they are excused until nine o'clock tomorrow morning. Court is at recess."

He banged that gavel of his and left the bench. Brunelle frowned at Edwards.

"I'm really sorry, Dave." She shrugged. "Brain fart."

"No worries," he replied. He was actually glad for the development. His cross had been going nowhere. Maybe he'd think of something effective overnight. "I'll see you tomorrow, rested and ready to kick your doc's ass."

Edwards shook her head and smiled. "Don't be so cocky, Dave. I think you may need some psychoanalysis of your own."

Brunelle grinned. "No time for that, Jess. I have an innocent woman to put in prison."

Adrianos was listening to every word.

CHAPTER 37

Arkham Asylum had nothing on Cascade Mental Hospital, at least not at twilight, the turrets and gables casting long shadows over the barred windows of the sanitarium. Brunelle parked his car in the same spot, the gravel crunching even louder in the silence that stuck to the scene like the new dew forming on the grass. He shut his car door and walked slowly to the heavy wooden door that was the border between the sane world outside and the insanity within. A moment later he was walking into the insanity.

Again, there was no receptionist. Again, One-Eyed Eddie sat on a bench to his left. If he was rocking, it was imperceptible. Brunelle wondered if he was sleeping. He wondered how much more violently Eddie would react to a bell that woke him from a deep sleep.

Mercifully, he didn't have to find out. Adrianos came swiftly down his hallway to the lobby. Brunelle looked up and saw the video surveillance camera blinking at him from a corner.

"Mr. Brunelle." He was on Brunelle in a flash, shaking his hand and steering him by the shoulder back toward his office.

"Thank you for coming in. I'm sorry about all the confusion."

Brunelle shrugged as his shoes clacked off the institutional floor. "That's okay. It happens."

Adrianos looked down at him. "Does it happen a lot?"

"Discovery violations?" Brunelle answered. "I guess so. It's not supposed to, but we all have a lot of cases and—"

"No," Adrianos interrupted. "I mean you being confused. Does that happen a lot?"

Brunelle frowned. "I wasn't confused. Jessica made a mistake."

Adrianos offered a grin as they reached his office. "You avoided my question, Mr. Brunelle. Well done."

Brunelle looked at him. "I don't think I did."

"You don't?" Adrianos said as they stepped into his office. "That's interesting."

He gestured at the guest chairs. "Have a seat."

"I'd rather stand," Brunelle replied. It was uncomfortably quiet in the hospital. There were no sounds save their voices. He almost would have preferred some background screaming, or at least moaning.

Adrianos smiled sideways at him as he opened his file cabinet. "Interesting," he repeated. He pulled a file out and closed the drawer.

"Here you are, Mr. Brunelle." He handed the file to Brunelle.

Brunelle opened it and flipped through, looking for a report he didn't recognize. It was in the back. Only a few pages, but still, Edwards should have given it to him before she called Adrianos to the stand. Brunelle frowned at that, and also at his realization he wasn't going to be able to leave quite yet.

"There are no discs," he observed. "You couldn't transfer the video, huh?"

"No," Adrianos answered. "We have a proprietary system. All of our videos can be viewed on our system, but it's not compatible with other players." He raised an eyebrow at Brunelle. "I mentioned that in court today. Did you forget?"

Brunelle shook his head. "No, I was just hoping I could get out of here sooner rather than later."

"Oh." Adrianos nodded. "Is someone expecting you?"

"No," Brunelle answered too quickly. "I don't have any plans tonight. I just don't like to spend my free time in mental hospitals."

"Are you feeling uncomfortable?"

"I'm just looking forward to getting home," Brunelle replied brusquely. He was getting tired of the psychobabble. "Can we just watch the videos? Maybe I'll watch the most recent one first. I might not need to see the others."

He'd memorized the first two reports already anyway. The sooner he could get out of Chez Adrianos the better.

And for the third time, Adrianos said, "Interesting."

Brunelle wished he'd stop saying that.

"The video viewing room is in the forensic wing." Adrianos pointed toward the door. "Shall we?"

Brunelle nodded. "By all means."

He closed the file and followed Adrianos into the hallway. The echoes of their synchronized steps filled the corridor.

"You did a good job today," Adrianos said without looking at him.

"Oh, uh, thanks," Brunelle replied. He didn't usually get feedback from his witnesses, especially not in the middle of their testimony.

"You're a very good lawyer."

Brunelle nodded cautiously. "Thanks."

"That's fairly normal for narcissists," Adrianos observed.

"They are usually very good at what they do, and receive praise for it. It's when the amount of praise they need reaches an unhealthy level that one can begin to see the pathology behind the competency."

"Uh, okay," Brunelle answered. "I think I'm doing fine, thanks. I like what I do. I don't need praise."

"We all need praise," Adrianos countered. They had reached a heavy metal door which separated the administrative wing from the forensic wing. Adrianos entered a code into the keypad and the clang of the bolt unlocking echoed through the hallway.

Brunelle shrugged. "Sure. But I know I'm good at what I do. I don't need people telling me that all the time."

They stepped through the door and it slammed shut behind them. It seemed even quieter in the forensic wing, Brunelle thought, if that were even possible.

"Well, what about the opposite?" Adrianos asked. "Are you afraid of losing this case?"

"Not afraid," Brunelle replied. "Anxious, but not afraid."

"Anxious?" Adrianos repeated. "That's interesting. What are you anxious about?"

Brunelle tapped the file folder. "A murderer might go free."

"What about losing face? Status? Respect?"

Brunelle shook his head. "No, I'm confident in my abilities. This is a difficult case. If I lose, I lose. But if I win—"

"Then you really are a great lawyer," Adrianos finished his sentence, and came to a stop in front of another metal door. "Right?"

Brunelle stopped too and looked Adrianos in the eye. He really hated psychologists. "Right," he admitted.

Adrianos raised an eyebrow. "And if you lose the case, you might lose your job."

Brunelle grimaced. "You heard about that, huh? I'm not too

worried. Like I said, I do a good job."

"Of course you do," Adrianos said as he entered another code into this next keypad. "But sometimes, it's that one extra fear that can send us over the edge."

"I'm not going over any edge," Brunelle assured him.

"If you lose your job," Adrianos ignored Brunelle protest, "you lose your identity. You won't be a prosecutor any more. You won't be the hero any more."

"I won't be able to eat any more," Brunelle quipped, uncomfortable with Adrianos' two-minute psycho-assessment of his life.

The door unlocked with another armored clank and Adrianos opened it, gesturing Brunelle to walk in first. "So, you're confused, forgetful, anxious, and about to lose your hero identity."

Brunelle turned back and frowned. "I didn't say that," he was pretty sure. "You did."

Adrianos stood in the doorway. "Do you know what a D.M.H.P. is, Mr. Brunelle?"

Brunelle had heard the acronym. They had them in the jail for the crazy inmates. His expression must have betrayed his uncertainty.

"It stands for Designated Mental Health Professional," Adrianos explained. "I'm a D.M.H.P."

Brunelle nodded slowly. "Okay."

Adrianos stepped up to Brunelle. Brunelle was reminded of the several inches and dozens of pounds Adrianos had on him.

"A D.M.H.P. has the authority to detain someone who is undergoing a psychotic episode," Adrianos said. Brunelle suddenly noticed there was no video-viewing equipment in the room. In fact there was nothing in the room at all. Adrianos grabbed him by the shoulder and he felt a sharp prick at the base of his neck.

Brunelle grabbed his neck and stumbled backward. He felt a rush of heat into his face and extremities.

"You're having a narcissistic break, Mr. Brunelle," Adrianos said as he stepped back into the hallway, the hypodermic needle now obvious in his hand. "I can't let an innocent woman be convicted by a man who is having a psychotic breakdown."

Adrianos clanked the door shut as Brunelle felt his legs weaken. He dropped to one knee.

"Just try to relax, Mr. Brunelle," Adrianos' voice came over a loudspeaker. "You need rest. A nurse will be by in the morning to administer more meds."

The heat in Brunelle's extremities was turning into an all-over warmth. It engulfed the beat of his heart and the stream of his thoughts. He was only minimally aware of the room going dark before he slumped to the floor and passed out.

CHAPTER 38

Brunelle knew he'd dreamt, but he couldn't remember the dreams. Somehow, he knew to be glad for that. But his head was still thick with whatever Adrianos had stuck into his neck, so when the door clanked open and a ray of light fell across his face, he was pretty sure he was still dreaming. Or else he was dead.

Looking up he guessed the latter. There was an angel kneeling down next to him.

"Dave," said the angel. "Dave, wake up. Are you okay?'

Brunelle forced his eyes to focus on the scarred face in front of his. It was Robyn.

'Robyn,' he tried to say. It came out as "Rrrgghhnmm."

She helped prop him into something resembling a sitting position. His limbs felt like lead.

"Breathe deeply," Robyn told him. "You'll feel better in a few minutes."

"Whunngh?" Brunelle tried. He took a breath and focused on

making his tongue work. "What happened?"

"Peter injected you with a narcotic," Robyn explained. "He thinks you're insane."

Brunelle, with some conscious effort, managed to swallow. Then he nodded heavily. "Takes one to know one."

His wits were returning to him. "Hhnn—How did you find me?"

Robyn looked down. "Peter likes to celebrate his victories," she said.

Brunelle shook his head at her. He didn't understand.

"He talks in his sleep," she expounded.

"Ah." He got it. "Celebrate. You. Bed. Sleep. Got it."

He tried not to puke.

"You need to get out of here before the nurse comes," Robyn stood and started to pull him to his feet. "She does her rounds at nine."

"What time is it?" Damn, that light from the hallway was bright.

"Not quite eight. Enough time to get to the courthouse before she finds you missing and calls Peter."

Brunelle nodded. It hurt less than the last time he moved his head. That was good.

She handed him his wallet and keys. "I couldn't find your phone," she apologized, "but Peter left these in his desk. Now get out of here."

Brunelle didn't need to be told twice. Well, apparently he did need to be told twice. But not three times.

He took his keys and wallet and staggered into the hallway. His head was clearing. He remembered something important to say. "Thank you, Robyn."

She smiled. He loved that dimple of hers. "You're welcome.

Now go."

Three times after all. He was a stubborn bastard. As Adrianos was about to find out.

CHAPTER 39

Brunelle would later blame it on the drugs still in his system, but as he exploded into Perry's courtroom, he realized he hadn't thought things out quite enough. For starters, he looked like hell. This was confirmed by the expressions of shock he received from those inside the courtroom—a shock exceeding that warranted simply by the courtroom doors banging open. He also had a vague awareness that he might not have smelled all that good either. He realized he didn't need to use the bathroom, and didn't recall any toilet in his cell. That left only one unappealing conclusion as to where he had last urinated.

But more than all that, he realized he hadn't called Chen or anyone else in advance. He hadn't even recruited the security guards as he passed the metal detectors at the front entrance. Instead, he had gone directly to the courtroom and stormed in, probably looking just about as crazy as Adrianos claimed he was.

All of which meant, when that happened, and everyone stopped whatever they were doing—like the scene in the Old West bar where the piano player stops playing and everyone looks at the gunslinger who just walked through the swinging door—there were only two people who actually knew what was going on: Brunelle and Adrianos, the man who'd risked everything to kidnap him. Everyone else stood there, momentarily stunned.

Which gave Adrianos just enough time to grab the gun from the holster of the corrections officer standing next to him.

Sometimes, narcissists just need one more thing to snap.

The corrections officer reached for his belt, but it was too late. He stepped toward Adrianos, just as the two other officers unholstered their own weapons—and Adrianos grabbed Edwards as a shield. He put the gun to her neck and backed up, looking around wildly.

Perry wasn't on the bench yet. The bailiff hit the alarm and he and the court reporter ducked behind the bar. Brunelle heard the door to the judge's chambers lock from the inside. The two reporters in the front row ran out the main door. Thompson, who'd come to watch Adrianos testify again, crouched down between the gallery benches. Fargas, that bastard, hadn't arrived yet. And the unarmed officer abandoned Adrianos, and instead secured his prisoner, pulling Keesha away from the gunman and handcuffing her to a chair in the back corner.

The standoff was complete.

"Let her go," Brunelle tried to command. He didn't slur his speech, but there wasn't much force to his voice either.

"Why?" Adrianos answered. "She's my only chance of getting out of here alive."

Good point, Brunelle admitted to himself. Instead he said, "You're not getting out of here period. You know that. Don't make this any more serious than it already is."

A good counterpoint, he thought.

Adrianos seemed to think so too. His mind was racing

behind wild eyes. "Damn you, Brunelle. How did you get out?"

He was thinking clearly enough to say, "I'm not telling you that."

But it didn't matter.

"I let him out." Robyn walked into the courtroom. She stepped around Brunelle and right up to Adrianos and the understandably silent Edwards.

"You two-timing slut," Adrianos growled. "I never should have trusted you."

"You didn't, Peter," she replied. "You never did. But you talk in your sleep and you're too proud for your own good."

"So you let your new boyfriend out. Fine. Another fuck-toy for you. You never were anything more than a common whore."

"I'm an uncommon whore," she said. Then, her voice lowered just a notch. "I'm your whore."

That was an unexpected turn in the conversation, but then again, the last twenty-four hours had been pretty unexpected. But the comment jarred Brunelle from merely observing the scene to analyzing it. He noticed that no additional officers had arrived. Undoubtedly they had been called. He supposed they had set up a perimeter and were guarding all possible exits. Which meant they were guarding all possible entrances too. But Robyn had been let through. *'I can be very convincing.'*

It was a set up.

"Peter," she said. "Let Jessica go. She had nothing to do with this. Take me instead. You'll still get out of here. Then we can talk."

Adrianos didn't say anything. He looked at Edwards, who was trying not to hyperventilate with a .45 caliber semi-automatic shoved under her jaw, then at Robyn again.

"Put the gun to my neck, Peter," she said. "Let her go."

"You'd like that, wouldn't you?" Adrianos sneered. "You

pretend you like that stuff, but you don't really. You pretend I'm in control, but I'm not. It's really you. Always you. Just like all women."

This isn't going well, Brunelle thought. But for some reason he had faith in Robyn.

"Let her go, Peter," she repeated, taking a step toward him. "Take me. You won't hurt me. That's our deal, remember? You never really hurt me."

Robyn reached out and pulled Edwards from Adrianos' grasp. He didn't resist. She pushed Edwards to the side and took her place in front of Adrianos, her back against his chest, the gun against her dimple. Adrianos let her do it. He was right: she was in charge.

She looked up at him. "Ready, Peter?"

He nodded. "Yes. I'm ready."

"Me too," she breathed, and reached up to kiss him. Adrianos hesitated, but then leaned into the kiss. That's when she bit down on his lip and tore away, blood spurting across her dimple.

"You bitch!" he yelled and shoved her away.

Brunelle didn't know if he'd pushed her away just out of blind rage, or to line up the kill shot he was going to take on her. But it didn't matter.

Robyn was clear.

The officers opened fire.

FIRST EPILOGUE

"Not guilty by reason of insanity?" Kat asked over Brunelle's glass. She was trying some of his whiskey. "Do you think that's justice?"

Brunelle nodded. They were at the same bar as the night he hadn't gotten any dinner. Not that he was complaining.

"I always did." he said. "She's insane. She belongs in a mental hospital, not prison. After the first trial ending in a mistrial—that happens when the star defense witness goes nuts and gets shot dead in the courtroom—Jessica was in no mood to try the case again. Especially without Adrianos to bullshit the jury. Besides, no other psychologist wanted to validate that nut job's opinions, so she really had no choice. We drafted up an agreed NGRI judgment and Keesha will spend the next twenty years at Western State Hospital where she can get the help she needs."

"What about Fargas and his lawsuit?" Kat slid the glass back to Brunelle. "And your job?"

Brunelle grinned and took his own sip of his drink. "That was the best part. With no jury verdict, Fargas will actually have to prove up his own case. We didn't get in his way, but we didn't do his work for him either. And after everything that happened, there was no way anyone was going to fire me."

"Oh yeah?" Kat asked. "How come?"

"Because I'm crazy, remember?" he laughed. "If they fire me now, it's discrimination. I'll hire Fargas and sue the shit out of the county."

"Very nice," Kat raised her wine glass in a toast. Brunelle clinked it and they both drank. Then she looked around. "Are you starving, David?"

Brunelle assessed his gut. "No, I guess not. Why?"

Kat rubbed the back of her neck. "We've had a rash of bodies lately. I'm doing six autopsies a day easy. I'm pretty stressed."

Brunelle grinned. "You need some stress relief?"

She batted her eyelashes at him. "Would you mind?"

"Of course not." He stood up and placed some money on the bar. "If I don't take care of you, someone else will."

SECOND EPILOGUE

It was two weeks later when Robyn tracked Brunelle down at his office. Almost quitting time again, but not quite. When the receptionist buzzed him to tell him that a Robyn Dunn had come by to see him, he dropped what he was doing like a hot potato and hurried to the lobby.

"Robyn," he said smoothly as he opened the door to the sitting area. "What a nice surprise. What brings you by?"

He hoped it was something that might take a while. It wasn't.

"I finally found your phone," she said, pulling the device from her small purse. She held it out to him. "Here."

"Oh." Brunelle took it. "Great. Thanks."

Robyn smiled. "I added my number to your contacts."

That's more like it, he thought. "Oh yeah?"

"Yeah." She grinned. "I wanted you to know who the text was from."

Brunelle cocked his head at her, not immediately understanding the comment.

"Bye, Mr. B," she said with a wave. "Hope to see you again soon."

Then she walked out of the lobby and toward the elevators.

Brunelle watched after her, then looked down at the phone. He touched the screen to light it up. He had one new text. From 'Rrrobyn D.'

When he read it, his heart raced almost as fast as his mind.

'I'll never say no.'

END

THE DAVID BRUNELLE LEGAL THRILLERS
Presumption of Innocence
Tribal Court
By Reason of Insanity
A Prosecutor for the Defense
Substantial Risk
Corpus Delicti
Accomplice Liability
A Lack of Motive
Missing Witness
Diminished Capacity
Devil's Plea Bargain
Homicide in Berlin
Premeditated Intent
Alibi Defense
Defense of Others

THE TALON WINTER LEGAL THRILLERS
Winter's Law
Winter's Chance
Winter's Reason
Winter's Justice
Winter's Duty
Winter's Passion

ALSO BY STEPHEN PENNER
Scottish Rite
Blood Rite
Last Rite
Mars Station Alpha
The Godling Club

ABOUT THE AUTHOR

Stephen Penner is an attorney, author, and artist from Seattle.

In addition to writing the *David Brunelle Legal Thriller Series*, he is also the author of the *Talon Winter Legal Thrillers*, starring Tacoma criminal defense attorney Talon Winter; the *Maggie Devereaux Paranormal Mysteries*, recounting the exploits of an American graduate student in the magical Highlands of Scotland; and several stand-alone works.

For more information, please visit *www.*

Made in the USA
Las Vegas, NV
24 July 2023

75201193R00125